Zach sat next to Kim, and before she knew what was happening, he had her on his lap

She squealed, but his lips were against hers in a kiss so hungry he thought he might have hurt her. He tried to pull away, but her arms went around his neck, and she held on to him. "You'd better not start something and not finish," she whispered.

"I wouldn't think of it."

He pulled the pins from her hair and pitched them onto the floor. "Zachary," she protested lightly, "I need those for later."

"Too bad," he said as he pulled the last one from the bun, and then he unwound it and let the soft strands of hair spiral into his palm. Kim let her head fall back and he drove his fingers through her hair from her scalp all the way to the soft ends. She purred and he bit her neck. Kim dissolved in his arms, curling into him. "You're going to make me be very bad, Zach," she said, her mouth against his neck where she licked him.

"Baby, sometimes, bad is good."

Books by Carmen Green

Kimani Romance

This Time for Good
The Perfect Solitaire
The Perfect Seduction
That Perfect Moment

CARMEN GREEN

was born in Buffalo, New York, and had plans to study law before becoming a published author. While raising her three children, she wrote her first book on legal pads and transcribed it onto a computer on weekends before selling it in 1993. Since that time, she has sold more than thirty novels and novellas, and is proud that one of her books was made into a TV movie in 2001, *Commitments,* in which she had a cameo role.

In addition to writing full-time, Carmen is now a mom of four and lives in the Southeast. You can contact Carmen at www.carmengreen.blogspot.com or carmengreen1201@yahoo.com.

That Perfect
MOMENT

CARMEN GREEN

KIMANI ROMANCE

That Perfect Moment is dedicated to
Trevor Malcolm McCray for being an ardent supporter
forever. And to the sparrow for always having my back.
I miss you.

KIMANI PRESS™

ISBN-13: 978-0-373-86222-1

Recycling programs
for this product may
not exist in your area.

THAT PERFECT MOMENT

Dear Reader,

The Hoods are the best, aren't they? I wanted to create a family of men and women who worked hard at being good and doing good for everyone. They are the law and order we dream about—upstanding people who would risk their lives for what's right—and they're sexy, too. What an awesome combination.

I hope you enjoy Zach Hood's story. He's *so* easy to fall in love with.

Thinking of you,

Carmen Green

Thank you to The Art Institute of Atlanta-Decatur Fashion Department, most especially Tonya Felton and Chanel Thorpe for making me look wonderful for my photo shoot. Also, special thanks to Professor Courtney Hammond for all his sage advice. To my photographer, Marie Williams of Top Studios, I very much appreciate your ability to make me look so wonderful. To my family: Jeremy, Danielle and Christina, my parents, and brothers and sisters, always amazing, always in my heart. Finally, to the team of doctors, nurses and everyone else who put me back together again, and continue to work with me, I thank you all so very much for everything.

Chapter 1

Everyone in the courtroom waited in tense anticipation of the sentence Judge Kimberly Thurman was about to hand down to the serial carjacking teenager who'd had no regard for his victims. She referred to the paperwork in front of her, then asked the impudent defendant to stand.

Security specialist and part owner of Hood Investigations Incorporated, Zachary Hood sat in the last row of the gallery of the nearly empty courtroom and watched the judge's reaction to the young man. With her hands folded, she leaned forward, her shoulders making her robe look stately, as she ignored his insolence. Her hair, which he knew was long and straight, had been pulled into a tight bun, accenting a regal face, allowing long platinum earrings to highlight her beauty. Her eyelashes were long and black, and fanned defined cheekbones that had been subtly dusted with bronzer.

Zach noticed every detail. His job was to miss nothing, and he took pride in it. His attention was brought back to the young defendant as the judge waited for him to finish adopting his wide-legged—head cocked to the side—stance of defiance. She didn't even bother to comment when he intentionally smacked his hands together in front of himself as a general sign of disrespect to her, and the court.

The male deputies showed more annoyance than she. "Thaddeus Drake Baxter," the judge began with a firm tone. "The sentencing recommendation of eighteen months in jail with six months for time served has been rejected by the court. You are hereby sentenced to seventeen years in prison to be served at a state facility to be determined by the State of Georgia Department of Corrections. This sentence is to be served concurrently." The judge then read several case numbers to the clerk of the court, and the year breakdown for each violation.

She then looked Thaddeus Drake Baxter in the eye, and that's when Zachary saw a flicker of regret. It was there and gone so fast, but he knew he hadn't missed it.

"This is the judgment of the court, so say we one and all."

The defendant's family reacted with screams of protest. "For carjacking? That's insane," his mother wailed. The rest of the family sobbed. Four Baxter men glared at her, one shouting profanely.

The gavel's sharp rap against the pad caught everyone's

attention. "Quiet in the courtroom!" The judge's calm demeanor vanished. The gripped gavel was pointed directly at the family. "The evidence was presented and a verdict delivered. You knew this day was coming, Mrs. Baxter. The citizens of this state and the court system did what you weren't able to do—control your son. He won't hurt another woman for a very long time, if ever again."

The stunningly beautiful judge peered over the bench at the large male members of the Baxter clan and didn't flinch.

Every male in a position of authority was poised to protect the judge, although she seemed able to handle herself. Still, Zach, himself, would have vaulted seven rows to subdue the Baxter men.

"This is wrong, dead wrong," the largest of the uncles said. His face in profile, he looked more feral than the rest of them. The elder Baxter looked like he'd raised hell in his day, and had matched it blow for agonizing blow. A healed wound was etched into his face like Interstate 75 was in Georgia's highway infrastructure. His nose had been broken several times, and his dark eyes were flat. His face showed the knocks and bruises of a man who hadn't ever been able to control himself; he still lacked that ability.

He stood in the second row, but leaned over the back of the first row as if that would get him closer to the judge. "You gon' get—" he threatened.

The judge banged the gavel, cutting him off just as a deputy wrenched the man's arm behind his back, slapping the cuffs onto his wrist in a quick move. Out of instinct, Zach had risen and advanced.

Baxter's roar of pain was that of a lion, and it cut through the silence in the courtroom.

The judge was the only one who spoke. "If you finish that sentence, you will be arrested and charged with threatening an officer of the court, and making terroristic threats." Her eyebrow inched up and Baxter blew air through his nose.

"Your bail will be set at two-hundred and fifty thousand dollars. When you are convicted, you will serve day for day of your sentence in a federal prison. Now that you fully understand the implications of your words, Mr. Baxter, do you have anything else you'd like to say to me?"

Zach had moved against the wall, and while he didn't have his gun, he didn't feel he needed it in a room full of sheriff deputies and Baxter men. It would be a brawl if they started anything. The family looked that unpredictable. Baxter's teeth were bared as he glared at her, his family stunned and quiet. The hell seeped out of him like sweat off moist skin. His brother reached back and pulled him by the middle of his shirt, and gave a stilted nod of apology to the judge.

The deputy who had detained Baxter looked at the judge and she gave a barely noticeable signal to release him. The family quietly left the courtroom.

Amazed that the man had even tried to disrespect the judge in that manner, Zach turned his attention back to the defendant. His posture of bravado was gone, and he was now a lost nineteen-year-old, leaning on his attorney, sobbing. The young man was led away, the tension, however, taking longer to dissipate.

Despite being thirty-four, two years his senior, the judge looked younger than her years. Zach didn't think Judge Thurman remembered meeting him at the four-day course he'd taught on safety for members of the High Court. That conference had been two years ago. At that time she'd been vehemently opposed to judges carrying weapons, but that had been before the Courthouse Shooter had struck Atlanta, Georgia. Today, Judge Thurman looked like she could handle anything thrown her way. He slid open the paper he'd received and read it again. *Someone is trying to kill me. I need your help.* Obviously, she was in trouble.

The judge dismissed court, and everyone stood until she left the bench. An aide led Zach to her outer office and he sat, taking everything in. The double glass doors leading to her inner sanctum could be accessed by an electronic key card. The simplicity of the outer office appealed to him. There were only two assistant's desks, with visitor's chairs that were placed ten feet away from the desks, for privacy's sake.

Zach waited, his thoughts returning to the judge. He could see why someone would want to kill her, but he couldn't imagine anyone being bad enough to try. Excitement coursed through his body like an energy drink, and he welcomed the adrenaline. This feeling didn't happen often and when it did, he took notice. He was going to win this account, but first he had to hear what the judge had to say.

Zach stood just as the door opened. "The judge will see you now."

Chapter 2

Judge Kimberly Thurman made being a Superior Court judge look sexy as she sat in her office on Courtland Street in Atlanta, Georgia. There was no boxy brown desk, with the obligatory picture frames of cats or kids covering the wooden space. Her desk was made of clear beveled green glass, accented with a computer that was built into the flat surface. The judge sat cozily on a sofa of Italian leather in an alcove in front of a window so she could catch the soft afternoon sunlight.

Zach was escorted in by her assistant Clark. "Your Honor? Do you mind moving over here?" Zach asked. If there was a threat against her, he wanted her to live long enough to tell him about it. Sitting by the window as she was, she was in a direct firing path should a sniper choose to access the roof of the building across the street. It didn't matter that the building was police headquarters. Anything was possible.

"I'm glad you're taking my concerns so seriously. Do you think someone is out there now?" The judge stood and moved.

"Having you move is just a precaution. Finding out would be my business. I don't know if you remember me. We met at the four-day Symposium on Judges' Safety two years ago. Hood's position was that judges needed self-defense training and to improve safety in your travels from work and home. Your families needed to be more aware of safety issues, also."

Loneliness lifted her lips in a soft tilt as she brushed her fingers against her cheek. "I remember you. I was opposed to judges carrying guns on the bench. My views have changed, given the events that have taken place in our city. The self-defense course you taught got all the female judges talking."

Zach chuckled. "Did it?"

"Yes, sir, it most certainly did." She smiled back. "That's when I checked out Hood Investigations. Your outfit was hired because it was an impartial third party. A couple years ago, there was a big murder case, and members of our elite police units were going before several of us judges. Officers were put in jail, and Atlanta was thrust into the national spotlight.

"When the symposium came about, they decided against using our own officers for training because they didn't want to mix our police with the judges. They didn't want there to be even the hint of impropriety. For the record, I've taken concerns about my safety to the chief twice, and he's all but patted me on the head and told me to go away. I'm not begging him to help me. Once I knew Hood was a legitimate security company and that your success rate was one hundred percent, I wanted to hire you."

"I remember you from self-defense class. You beat the hell out of my dummy."

Kim burst out laughing. "That's what he was there for."

Zach nodded, relaxing a bit, thinking back. "We met again six months ago, Judge."

Kim thought for a moment. "I don't recall."

"I appeared in your courtroom."

Her eyes clouded and disappointment crashed in like the surf. "Oh, no."

"It's not what you think. I wasn't in trouble. We worked marathon court. The great Fulton County backlog."

Kim pressed her hand to her mouth. "Oh, yes, I do remember you! What a nightmare that was. Three thousand cases. Oh, my goodness. The governor and the U.S. Attorney ordered the court system to process the cases within one month. How many fugitives did Hood bring before us?"

"We captured fifty of Atlanta's Missing and Wanted. We didn't sleep or eat for months before those fugitives had to appear in court. We went into hell to find those men and women." He snapped his fingers. "I remember your hair was shorter then. You yelled at me! My fugitive was talking in court, and you thought it was me."

They both started laughing.

Kim clasped her hands together. "I'd hoped you'd forgotten that. We were under a tremendous amount of pressure. Sorry," she said shyly.

"No worries. You were just doing your job."

"We all were. That's why I called for you, Zach. If you and Hood Investigations could find fifty people who didn't want to be found, you can find out who's trying to kill me. Can you help me?"

His gaze met hers, and he got lost in the yearning and the question there. She wanted to live, and she needed his help.

Zach found himself looking at the judge as a woman and not a client. He focused on the carpet and realigned his thoughts. Before he did something unprofessional, he pulled out his computer. "Yes, I believe we can. Let me tell you what Hood Investigations can do for you."

Zach pulled up the presentation that took less than ten minutes. "You would never be alone. There are four men on the team and three women. We work multiple cases, but in your case, we'd all work together due to the high priority."

"Because of my status as a judge?"

"Yes." Zach stopped the PowerPoint presentation from moving forward. "And, *you* called *us*. I know the marshals automatically provide security for you. But you have concerns for your safety, and that means you don't trust them implicitly. Second, if a judge has a cause for concern, and you're approaching Hood, you've gone through the regular channels and didn't get the results you wanted. Are you concerned about people like the Baxters?"

"On a minor level, but my concern is that the threats against me may have been an ongoing thing, and we ignored the initial signs. I don't want to sound paranoid."

Her confidence wavered and she looked so unsure of herself. So like a vulnerable woman. For years he'd been teaching women to follow their instincts; the only thing that had kept some of them alive. He had no doubt the judge believed someone was after her. He wondered if it was true.

There was a double knock at the door and the judge's assistant Clark walked in. Tall and well groomed, the thin man looked at his boss affectionately, then at Zach. "I had to eavesdrop on her, because I knew she wasn't going to tell you everything."

"What aren't you telling me, Judge Thurman?"

"Clark, don't make me look bad." Even as she said the words, she made room for him on the spacious couch. He sat near her and she touched his hand.

"She's going to get killed unless she's honest. Mr. Hood, I insisted she contact you. I was trying to protect Judge Thurman when we were attacked one night after dance class."

"Are you two a couple?" Zach asked, and couldn't help frowning, because Clark seemed far more feminine than he did masculine.

Clark closed his eyes, smiled and shook his head. The judge didn't look offended at all.

"No, but in my opinion, I'm the best thing that's ever happened to her."

Judge Thurman chuckled, her smile affectionate, friendly.

"That is, until someone broke my arm and I'm leaving for three weeks to Puerto Vallarta. I can't go on vacation until I know she's going to be taken care of." Clark looked at her, then Zach, with real concern in his eyes. "I may joke, but I'm very serious. Someone is trying to kill her and I'm worried."

Zach nodded. "Start at the beginning. Tell me everything."

"The judge only has just a few outlets of relaxation. Rocking the babies at the children's hospital, Chicago step dance classes and going up to Lake Lanier and taking out her boat. She doesn't have a steady anybody in her life, so last summer she took sailing lessons, but this year, I'm her dance partner."

Zach looked at the judge, who was watching Clark with a smile on her face. "Please tell all my business, Clark."

"He's going to know your underwear color before too long, believe me. Really, Judge, I want you to be alive when I get back. He needs to know how I feel."

She took a deep breath and looked at Zach, who instinctively knew Clark wasn't her attacker. His concern was genuine. "Clark's right, Judge," Zach said. "I'll be your bodyguard, your best friend—your everything—before this is over. And you, me. But your secrets will always be safe with me. Finish telling me what happened, Judge."

"Last Friday night we finished dance class about nine forty-five and stopped at Brickstone for ice cream. The next thing you know, two men grab me, and Clark starts beating them with a tire iron."

"Was this in the parking lot? Was it before or after you came out of the ice cream store?" Zach asked, looking at Clark's arm, then at the judge.

"After we exited."

"Did you notice them following you?"

"No," Clark said, looking guilty. "But we don't pay attention like we should. Sometimes we window-shop or get our nails done. We're really good friends as well as coworkers. We work well professionally, and the judge is a very private person. I respect that."

Zach looked at their nails and noticed the manicures. He nodded, then shook his head. "I understand the need for discretion, but you also have to trust someone, and that's Clark." She nodded. "Okay," Zach continued, "where'd the tire iron come from?"

"I keep it beneath the back of the driver's seat. Last year a man tried to rob me outside the gym, so I keep a weapon in my car and in the judge's car. Anyway, Friday, I got the car door open and got the tire iron, but the bigger man got it away from me. He hit me on my arm with such force, my arm broke. Luckily, I can scream pretty loudly, and the two employees that were in the ice cream store ran out. They threw chairs at the men and blew whistles. The other man who had the judge let her go, and they drove off in a green Explorer SUV."

"Did you get a tag number?"

"I told the police in the report just SO2. That's it. I call them every day and they tell me they have nothing."

Zach wrote down what was said. "No other witnesses?"

"It was very near closing time and everyone was gone. There were cars passing by on the road, but it could have looked like a lovers' quarrel." The judge rubbed Clark's injured arm.

"Please don't worry about me," she told her loyal assistant.

He smiled, but their relationship was one that was deeper than a mere office acquaintance. His genuine care had saved her life. "The ice cream store did have cameras embedded in the exterior walls. The video arrived today."

Clark moved to get up, but she patted his arm. She went to her desk and Zach watched her move. A black sleeveless, jewel-neckline dress hugged a shapely figure that was buxom on top, just the way he liked on a woman. Gold cuffs circled her wrists, while she wore a topaz on her right ring finger. While her hair had been in a conservative bun in court, she'd taken it down in her office, and she had freshened her lipstick, adding a shiny gloss.

In court, she hadn't smiled once, but inside the confines of the warmly appointed room with the cocoa-colored microsuede couch, red-and-sienna-colored pillows, he could see how this would be a place where she smiled and relaxed in peace before going home. Zach accepted the DVD from the judge and put it in his bag.

"Have there been other attacks?"

The judge nodded, taking her seat. "While I was

sitting in the hospital with Clark, I began to recall things. About a month ago, I got the impression some-one was following me as I drove around one weekend running errands. I deviated my plans and lost the car, but I never got over that feeling. I alerted the marshals, but with budget cuts, security is an area they trimmed. Without a valid, active threat that I could prove, I was pressured into releasing the extra security detail."

Zach took notes. "That's crap. This just happened Friday. You were threatened in court today. There should be security posted outside your office right now. Ridiculous," Zach told her.

Clark nodded. "I agree. I've contracted food poi-soning three times this year, and that's just crazy for it only being the ninth month of the year. I swear, I get poisoned every time Chef Henrietta comes here. I be-lieve it's her."

The judge's disbelieving look told Zach not to be-lieve Clark. "Clark, what do you think this is about?" Zach asked pointedly.

"I suspect it's jealousy or revenge. An envious col-league or a vengeful defendant or their family."

"That's an interesting viewpoint. No ex-employee or ex-lover?"

"No," Clark replied, followed quickly by a no from the judge.

"If an employee has a problem, they can come to me. I'm tough, but I'm not without a heart."

"In your opinion, Your Honor," Zach pushed, test-ing her temper.

Kim didn't take the bait. "It could be a stranger. I just wonder why?"

"It's not a stranger," Zach said quietly. "But we'll find out who it is and end it. That's what Hood does."

"I like that," Clark said.

"If I had to ask you for five names of suspects, who would they be?" Zach had directed the question to Clark, but Kim tried to intercept it, seeming to hate not being in control.

"That's not fair," Kim cut in.

"Judge, with all due respect, I'm trying to catch someone who is assaulting you. Nothing is impossible. Let him answer."

"Trevor is the second assistant, and I think he's rather sketchy. Lieutenant Franklin. Howard Daniels is a sheriff. The Baxters." His eyes widened as he talked. "And Merrill O'Dell was the judge's first conviction ten years ago, but he won an appeal recently. He skipped probation and hasn't been seen since."

Pleased, Zach wrote down everything Clark said, while Kim managed to look surprised and slightly annoyed.

"I believe Trevor is harmless," she countered.

"Then where is he?" The sarcastic twist to Clark's mouth wasn't lost on Zach. "He's gone longer than anyone on break, he leaves early all the time, and I've put him on two action plans for shoddy work. The man is a terrible assistant. He needs to be fired, yet you won't do it." He eyed the judge. "In my humble opinion," he added, then rolled his eyes.

"He's not that bad of an assistant, and he's entitled

to be absent once in a while. We all work hard and sometimes people have private lives that require some leeway. I don't believe Trevor is a threat, but you're going to do your own investigation."

Zach nodded. "That's right."

Clark hugged the judge, then stood, holding his healing arm as he walked to the office door. "I'm going on three weeks of vacation far away from here, and when I get back I expect things to be different." He smiled and leaned toward Zach. "Puh-lease. I don't want to die."

Zach chuckled, shaking his head. "You're not going to die, and not a hair will be harmed on the judge's head, either. You remind me of Daniel, my administrative assistant. Nothing but drama."

Clark's eyes brightened. "Daniel? Well, I'd better cut your office a check. I'll drop it off to Daniel on my way out of town."

Zach looked at the judge, who seemed totally relaxed. Her legs were crossed and she was resting her face on her finger and thumb. "We haven't decided to do business yet," Zach told him, his gaze shifting back to the judge.

Clark held the doorknob. "Judge?" he asked softly.

She looked at the Hood Inc. logo that spun in a circle on Zach's computer. "Notify me when I am able to sign the contract, then cut a check for twenty thousand dollars to Hood Investigations. Also, prepare a dossier on all the marshals who've worked the security detail for the past twelve months."

"I'm going to need one on the staff, including you, Clark."

"Yes, sir."

Zach focused on the judge.

"Thank you and enjoy your holiday," the judge told Clark.

"Mr. Hood, everything is already compiled. I'll have it in a few minutes, then I'm leaving, okay, Judge?"

The judge waved and the door closed softly. She exhaled a deep breath. "I'm going to miss him."

"You'll be down an assistant for a few weeks. Can you manage?"

She looked confident. "I haven't forgotten how to type. It's not that we as judges can't do those forms, we just have so much other work to do. If I get swamped, I can get Trevor to step up."

"So you *do* have confidence in him." Zach appreciated that she seemed to be taking everything in stride, but he wondered how many sleepless nights she'd had wondering when her predator would strike again.

"I do, but I understand Clark's trepidations. Trevor came in and tried to take his job. There's been some bad blood between the two of them."

"What's Trevor's last name?"

"Mason."

He studied her. "Otherwise, how are you holding up?"

There was a silence that he realized was her way of choosing her words. "I'm relieved to know this is under way. But I don't think it's a staff member." She looked unsure again.

"If you had to guess, who do you think it is?"

Her hand caressed from her thigh to her knee. "One of my security detail."

"Why?"

"They know my schedule. Professional and personal."

"Have you ever been romantically involved with anyone on the staff or in the court system? Anyone on your detail?"

She was shaking her head before he finished the question. "Never."

Her quick answer made him think she was lying or that she at least had something to hide. She was gorgeous and she had to know it. The judge was the kind of fine that gave drunk men hope that they could approach her and come up a winner. Regardless of her position or theirs, he knew she had broken a few hearts in the hallowed halls of Georgia Justice.

"How long have you been in the justice system, Judge?"

She seemed eager to debunk his questions about any preconceived notion he might have about her private life. "I've been here long enough to know every step I take is being watched by my subordinates, peers and the powers that be. I'm always professional. Period, the end. It's saved me a lot of grief and heartache that other colleagues haven't been so fortunate to avoid. I've sacrificed," she said, and the word echoed through his body. "But I made a choice to do that. There is no one, Mr. Hood."

She was too beautiful to be alone, but there were a lot of women in Atlanta like her. He suddenly felt very protective of her. Zach checked himself, putting distance between them. He busied himself by stowing his computer in his bag. "Okay. It is possible that you could have a jealous relative?"

She shook her head. "There's no one left but me."

He swung back to not believing her. How was it that he and his brothers were always meeting and falling in love with women who had no one in the world?

The saliva dried in his mouth and he saw the judge's eyes narrow. "What are you thinking? You're squinting at me," she said directly. Her gaze didn't waver as she read him as quickly as he'd read her. No woman had ever done that to him before.

Zach sidestepped the quick observation. "We may have to temporarily suspend your extracurricular activities until we neutralize whoever is after you."

"I can sacrifice dancing, but not the other two. No."

"I beg your pardon?"

"I can't bend on those. Judges live by a code of conduct that restricts our behavior. This code basically controls our lives. I've given up a lot of things," she said, scooting forward on the couch until she could stand. "I'm not causing harm to anyone or anything. I'll do everything else you say. I'll be totally under your control as long as I can rock the babies and go out on my boat."

"Judge—"

"When we're alone, it's Kim, please."

Was she tired of *what* she was?

The judge went to a mirrored wall, inserted a key and opened a door Zach had no idea was there. From inside she removed a large briefcase and a tailored white purse that was as sleek as it was expensive. "Mr. Hood—"

"Zach," he said, standing.

Opening the classy white bag, she pulled out a black band that she wound around her hair until it was in a professional bun again. She dipped into the bag once again and came out with a shiny black case. Opening it, she slid black sunglasses into her hand. Leaning over her desk, she electronically signed the contract before stowing her iPad in her bag.

"Zach, you have to make those two things happen or I'll find another security detail. I heard that Hood Investigations was the best. You not only get your man, but you make them pay without killing them. Between you, me and the wall, that's my brand of justice. If I go into hiding *and* they kill me, they win. Can you do the job?"

Zach didn't try to conceal his smile. She had become the judge again. Her logic was impeccable and refreshing. Women just didn't think like her. "We do whatever it takes to get our man."

She handed him her pashmina to drape over her shoulders, and when she turned, she was just beneath him. Kim's sensuality was as effortless as her beauty.

"Let me make this clear," Zach continued, denying himself the opportunity to be lulled by her feminine appeal. "If he gets too close, if anyone in your circle is endangered, you do it my way."

Her face was expressionless, and then he saw it. Respect sparkled like a firecracker on a hot July night. She covered her eyes in black sunglasses and her lips eased into a sexy smile. "You're the boss."

The words had never sounded sexier. Never sounded more provocative than they did right then.

"First, we're going to do background checks. Shake the trees and see what falls out."

Zach decided right then that he loved her eyebrows because they arched over her dark glasses and told him what her eyes would not. He got her safely into his SUV and they were under way quickly.

He made sure they weren't being followed, driving through the streets of Atlanta that he knew so well. Kim crossed her legs and he averted his gaze, vowing not to look again. If he was going to get the job done right, the last thing he needed was to want her. "You haven't told me something," Zach said. Her body language was different since they'd left the courthouse.

"I didn't want to mention this while Clark was still in the office. He would never have gone on vacation. This was on the gate when I drove to work this morning." She handed him a note.

Zach didn't want to pull over, but he had no choice. He broke protocol and stopped at a well-known restaurant parking lot and shifted the gears into Park, the car facing the street. He needed an easy escape route, if that became necessary. He pulled latex gloves from the glove box, a staple in his profession. "You should have told me earlier. I could have had this scanned and analyzed by now."

The note was simple. *You will feel my pain.*

It was impossible to tell whether the writer was male

or female, black or white, young or old. The one thing he could say was that they were smart. No unnecessary words. No clues, no hints at their next method of attack. Only the promise. These were the worst. Zach hated these perpetrators. Catching this one would take skill rather than strength. "On the gate of your house?" he asked.

"Yes. They couldn't get in," she assured him.

He nodded. They weren't professional. Not yet. "Don't keep anything else from me. We'll catch him that much sooner if I know everything. I hate surprises. They put us at a disadvantage."

She'd already pulled off her glasses.

Her gaze cut across the traffic, then back at him. "Get used to them. That's what law is all about. Managing the bad and evil surprises."

"I don't get used to anything. That's why I always get my man," he assured her. "Or woman." She crossed her left leg, then folded her arms. He knew what that meant. Off-limits. Women only clouded men's judgment, and he was there to work, only.

The judge had nothing to worry about. If her work ethic was as strong as she'd stated, his was made of carbonized steel.

Chapter 3

When was the last time a man had made Kim feel incompetent and unable to take care of a situation?

Zach pushed on the first-floor window in the sunroom, finding it unlocked. He frowned as he'd done a thousand times since they'd arrived at the house. He didn't like anything. Not her house, or the fact that it was a two-story and not a three-story. He made it clear that he thought her security system was inadequate and that she needed upgrades, including a dog, and he'd asked her more than once why was she single. As if she hadn't asked herself that a thousand times over the years until finally accepting the answer. She was meant to be alone.

Zachary Hood couldn't be made happy about anything. Kim had stopped trying. His expectations were too high. They'd slid into hour three of his interrogation fifty-nine minutes ago, and as hour four ticked away, she took a mental moment to figure out why her frustration level matched his. She had been happy with her life… Until she'd met him.

Kim wasn't sure what she'd expected, but it wasn't a judgmental man. She'd expected him to be more conciliatory. Someone who…well, acquiesced to her position as a judge. Someone who was at least nice.

Releasing the biggest sigh of the day, her tension eased a bit. It was the truth. It had been so long since anyone besides Clark told her she was wrong about something, and he was so gentle about it. Zach was trampling all over her tender feelings.

Kim slid her hand through her hair as they entered the keeping room, her mother's favorite room in the house she and Kim's father had owned before their deaths. This was the only room Kim had not changed when she'd had the house renovated a year ago. The curtains were still thick velvet brocade, and hung from heavy fourteen-foot rods, protecting stained-glass windows that dated back to the early nineteen hundreds, when the house had first been built.

The windows had been treated and re-stained, but that was all she'd had updated in the room.

"Wow, this is a throwback to the past," Zach murmured, more to himself than to her. His words weren't a criticism or snide, just a statement about the overall state of the room. It was mausoleum-like with the heavy dark furniture and the real Persian rugs. Kim knew that at some point she'd have to deal with the room and renovate. She'd have to deal with her feelings for her mother, too. Perhaps that was why the room was still in its untouched state, even after eight years.

Zach was ten feet into the room before he spoke. "Turn on the lights, please."

The lights were on a dimmer switch, and Kim tried to see the room as he did. The portrait that hung over the fireplace of her and her mother came into view as the lights grew brighter. Zach drew closer and studied her mom. "She was beautiful. You look just like her."

When more words didn't come, Kim became embarrassed.

"Thank you." The unexpected compliment had caught her off guard. Her heart hammered. She'd been called beautiful before, but she wanted to be respected by Zach.

She looked at her mother and her heart ached for the closeness they had lacked. For all that they hadn't been.

The sadness in the room overwhelmed her. "Are you almost finished? I can meet you in the library."

Zach had moved on, even as she walked toward the door, her heart beginning to race again. Anxiety from being in her mother's space was beginning to get to her. So many unshed tears. So many words unspoken.

"Come here," he said.

From above the fireplace, beautiful brown eyes gazed down at her and she looked away from Kay Thurman. Kim crossed the room to Zach, her jaw clenched. "Yes, Mr. Hood?"

"Were these windows ever fitted with security sensors?"

"No. The prickly bushes outside are so close to the

house, I didn't think a criminal would ever wade into them to get inside. They'd get sliced up."

Zach held back the thick curtain, and Kim waved dust out of her face. Then she saw what Zach was referring to. The beautiful stained-glass panes had been removed, leaving the window wedged open by six-inch blocks, waiting for whomever to return and finish the job of breaking into her house. They'd obviously wanted the expensive glass, because it was gone, but they wanted access, too. This was no smash and grab crime. This was methodical and thought out. There was no mistaking it. She was being targeted.

Her heart raced out of fear and stupidity. "Oh, my God. I didn't know." She reached out to snatch the blocks, and Zach caught her hand. Roughness met pampered softness.

"Get them out," she ordered. Panic hit her in the chest. "There was always a moment when I thought I was overreacting. I thought, they're not following me, are they? The attack on me was random. But this…this was meant for me. To get me."

"Kim, it's not the time to lose your head. If you needed confirmation, well, here's more proof. We're leaving the blocks in. We want him to think he's getting away with something. The truth is that the two incidents aren't related. There are two groups or people targeting you."

"What? How do you know?" As badly as she wanted to leave the room, Zach knew more than the chief of police or his deputies had told her in all her conversations with them.

"Anyone who leaves something on your gate can't get in. The note was intended to intimidate you. They want to show you their power, but they're showing their limitations. The person who got into this window could have gotten into the house, but something stopped them."

Fearful but curious, Kim had to ask all the questions racing through her mind. "Fear or something else?" She voiced her hope rather than her fear.

"Time and greed. He wants the glass, too," he said, feeding a fear so deep inside her she wanted to run. But nothing, not death or threats, had made her run in the past. She wouldn't run now.

"So they're still after me?"

"I believe whoever did this will try again. No one leaves a window open and doesn't return. They probably realized this glass is worth a lot of money, and they got sidetracked. They want it all. This is personal and potentially the most dangerous. I'm not quite sure yet."

"What are they doing with the glass? Keeping it as a trophy?"

Zach pursed his lips and shook his head confidently. He worked a piece free and slipped it into a plastic evidence bag. "No. The value is too high and too many are gone. They're selling it. It's heavy, so he could only carry a few at a time without being noticed. He's playing the law of averages. He'll be back, but he didn't count on you having better security. We will get this bastard. This one may have a smudge of blood on it."

"How soon will we know?" she asked, excited for the first time that day.

"A day or two." Zach remained hopeful. "How much was this glass?"

"They were ordered in bulk, but six hundred a piece. There about."

Zach grunted. "Stealing one is a felony. And he got six."

"Maybe he won't be back."

"Baby, you're a judge. He's gone undetected and he got away. This is an easy score for him. There are bragging rights for him right about now. He'll be back. There are two groups. I'm convinced of that."

Kim didn't know whether to believe Zach anymore. He'd been in her life for a few hours and she was so full of anxiety, she wasn't sure she trusted even her own judgment anymore. "I went from nobody believing me to having not one but two groups targeting me."

"Life's a bitch, ain't it?" Zach said, not looking at her, studying her alarm control panel. "You're just too close to it and you're the victim. I don't expect you to see things the way I do. No, wait." He smiled at her. "Yes, I do."

He disarmed her with that quick smile in the face of all this serious talk about her life. The thing was, she did believe him. And now, she was more afraid than ever.

"Why didn't the chief of police believe me?"

"Because he sent his best people to protect you, and if they investigated and said you were out of danger, then he would take their word over yours."

"What about Clark's arm and that attempted kidnapping? Surely that can't be swept under the rug?"

"No, it can't. I'll have my people follow up on that. I'll have answers for you, Kim. You never told me who has keys to your house."

His quick shift in conversation was a tactic used in trials to redirect witnesses, but Kim wasn't that easily distracted. She couldn't look away from the blocks wedging the window open. *Who would do this?*

It was well past nine, and the sun was finally fading for the evening, but a few rays still managed to reflect off the beautiful stained glass. Kim's heart ached for the mother who had neglected to love her. Zach was still waiting and Kim turned away from the glass to find his questioning gaze on her. "Lieutenant Jerome from the marshals has a key to the house. Clark, of course, and Flora, my housekeeper. Giuseppe, the grocery delivery man, and Paul, my next-door neighbor." She reached out again and Zach guided her away from the window. She finally met his gaze, unable to look away. "People are really trying to hurt me."

She was stuck, like a truck in the red Georgia clay after a hard rain. She wanted to ask Zach who would do this, but she couldn't. He didn't know any more than she.

"Five keys, huh? Why not leave a key in the mailbox with a note?" He tromped all over her already bruised feelings.

"I have no appreciation for sarcasm."

"I was kidding."

"No, you weren't."

"You're right. You're a judge, and you should have used better judgment. You've practically waved a flag at the satellites in space and said, 'notify all attackers, I'm waiting to be a victim.' How many doors open with that key that everyone has?"

Kim didn't really want to answer because he was right, of course. And since they had the key, they had the alarm code, too. It crossed her mind that she'd doled out her house key like French fries, and lots of keys could have been made. But why would those people betray her?

She braced for the onslaught of words her reply would bring. "All of the doors open with the same key." She knew he heard her barely audible words. She'd conceivably invited the perpetrator into her home.

"This house is how old?" he asked, saying nothing further, scrutinizing the glass on the window leading to the second floor.

"Ninety years old. It's been renovated twice. In the forties, and then a year ago. I have a bit of a defense for myself, Zach. When I'm home, I try to live a normal life. I didn't know I'd made myself so vulnerable."

"I don't really blame you, Kim. Your security team should be fired for not knowing about this. Then again, who knows when this happened? But this is how innocent people die."

"I've never had any trouble, and I've lived here for quite some time."

"You grew up in this house," he stated. How did he know? He'd only been in her house a few hours.

She thought about lying, but it would be useless. "How did you know?"

"The picture over the fireplace. I recognize the window behind the chair your mother is sitting in."

His astute observation was correct. The artist had captured only the side portion of the window, but Zach's attention to detail was uncanny. Men didn't usually notice much past her breast size and the fact that she was in a position of power.

"All my life, I went to boarding schools, and I visited here. After my parents died, I came back for good."

"I'm sorry. I didn't realize."

Zach sounded so sincere, Kim wished she hadn't brought it up. She never talked about her family or their less-than-close home life. She didn't need sympathy. She offered empathy only to those who genuinely needed it.

"There's nothing to be sorry about. This neighborhood was all but ignored by the young urban professionals who were buying up the land in the late nineties. Most of us second generation owners renovated and refurbished our family homes. We got lucky to have such nice property in the right zip code."

Zach gave her a wise, knowing look. "These houses are worth millions because of that zip code."

"The status associated with these is almost ridiculous." She waved nonchalantly.

"Why not leave if it makes you feel that way?"

"What way?" Kim crossed her arms and leaned away from him.

"Cold and detached."

"You don't know what you're talking about."

"I've touched a nerve. We don't have to talk about it. Let's move on."

He had more than touched a nerve. He'd run his six-foot-four self all over her central nervous system. Accepting the house had been a final thank-you for all of the years of boarding school, holidays alone and lonely nights. She'd taken it with bitter acceptance from their attorney at their graveside funeral. She, the child of spies, had hardly seen them.

Now she was living in their home, *her* home now, and being stalked as they used to stalk others for information. Kim shook off the ghosts of her parents, and needed coffee. Instead, she bit her nails; her one vice. At the door of the keeping room, Kim went ahead and walked out, hoping Zach would get the hint, but he ignored her.

"Why didn't you just sell?"

"I couldn't. As much as I disagreed with my folks, in their own way they loved me. I never told them how much they hurt me by not being home to care for me, but that hardly seemed the point when you're summoned to a hospital in the middle of the night to hear your mother's final words."

Zach didn't look at her. He simply stared at the floor and nodded. "I—understand. You're very lucky."

Kim hardly expected this. For Zach to become all maudlin and shake her unwavering opinion of her parents was unnerving. "I hardly feel that way."

"Sure, she was able to tell you how she really feels. It's so much better than getting that phone call and finding out she died alone."

You've been a wonderful daughter. Well done. Then she'd slipped away.

"What do I do now?" Kim rubbed her neck, ready to shut the door for another two years.

"We change everything. Locks, doors, bushes and windows. Why don't you have a dog?"

Kim felt herself frowning. "I'm never home, and a dog needs love."

An impertinent smirk crossed Zach's face, and Kim wanted to retract her answer. "No, they don't," he said. "They need food and commands on who and what to bite."

His phone buzzed and he walked out of the keeping room, into the library, ordering items for the house as if he were at a fast-food restaurant. Apparently, she needed a lot of number fours. Kim closed the door, hoping he'd shut the window. She had no plans to go in there again.

"Kim!"

Halfway to the kitchen, her chin hit her chest and she rolled her eyes. "I need coffee," she complained.

"Be strong," Zach told her from behind. "Set the alarm and come outside," he commanded, and waited for her on the outside steps.

Heading outside, Kim hurried up the cobbled walkway leading to the driveway.

"How many windows on the ground level?" Zach asked.

"Ten."

He relayed the information, then hung up. "This is going to be expensive to put bars up to the windows, but they are tasteful and will blend into the decor of the windows already on your home."

Shaking her head, Kim stopped walking. "No, I refuse to be imprisoned in my own home."

They walked the entire property, from the electric gate to the garage. Zach set and reset her sprinkler system. "Why are you doing that?" She was exhausted and hot. Knowing she'd contributed to people trying to hurt her made her sick. She just wanted to be left alone. "Zach?"

"The sprinkler is set to go on at four in the morning, but it's better to go on at nine in the evening."

"Why's that?"

He winked at her. "Easier to collect evidence at nine."

She shook her head. "You're lying to me."

He nodded, pointing to her bushes. "Yes, ma'am, I am. These flowers bloom between 4:00 and 5:00 a.m. If someone comes into the house and have stepped on these flowers, they leave quite a nice evidence trail. Though it's better when it's a dry trail. If it's wet, we can work with it, but it's harder to get out of the carpet."

Kim's eyebrow arched. "Oh."

Zach was proving to be far more than she'd expected. She shook her shoulders to lose her attitude. But bars up to the windows? The last thing she needed was to lower the property value of the neighborhood.

"Zach, I just can't have bars on my windows. It would make the wrong statement to the neighbors."

He nodded and guided her around by her elbow. "I understand. It's hot. Let's go inside."

The sprinkler system went off and Zach tried to dart out of the way, but still got soaked. Kim hurried to the front door and pushed it open to be greeted by a stranger with a gun in his hand.

She screamed and Zach shoved her into the house.

"Welcome home," the man said.

Shocked, Kim's mouth hung open. He was a Hood, she could tell, but he'd still scared the mess out of her. She was holding her heart, but Zach had his hand on the small of her back.

"My alarm should be going off." The words seemed inept, especially since everything was completely silent. Then the long beep sound started and Kim quickly disarmed it.

"Ben Hood," the stranger said. "Don't be afraid of me." He took her hand and rubbed it. Kim was actually embarrassed.

"Did you have to do a show and tell? I'm not a difficult learner," she said angrily. "I follow directions very well. You didn't need the visual effects. Are we finished? I've had a long day and I would like to relax."

"Not by a long shot," Ben continued. "Your alarm was active, but your motion detectors only work in certain rooms and only within a certain range. Did you know there's an anomaly with this particular system?"

Kim played with the gold cross around her neck. Could the day get any worse? she wondered. "What is it?"

"There can be movement in your home for up to five seconds and the alarm not activate."

"What?" she said in disbelief.

"This company is based out of California. They factored this feature in because of earthquakes. The average is just a few seconds long, so…"

Kim understood the logic, but didn't agree with it. "They didn't want the police to respond to false alarms, so they built in this five second rule." She shrugged as she stood there talking to who could have been her burglar. "If criminals only knew."

Ben gave her a knowing look. "Some do. But they're not fast, so they pick another house."

"I feel lucky," she said sarcastically. "How much are these updates and changes?"

Zach opened the front door again. "I will ignore your sarcasm. Look across the street." A man was waving from inside the neighbor's house. No one should have been there. The Sugarbakers had been on vacation in Spain for a month. "The height of your bushes allows a limited view of their home and them yours. If you need help, no one can come to your aid."

Even with his brother there, Zach was still by her side. "You've made your point. They're selfish neighbors for not inviting me to Spain while we get robbed, and my alarm company sucks, therefore they're fired."

Zach laughed and winked at her. "Smart lady." He dialed his phone and walked off, while the man who'd been in the Sugarbakers' house crossed the street and entered her house.

Kim extended her hand. "You're a Hood, too."

"Hugh Hood. Nice to meet you. It'll be expensive. About ten thousand dollars. You can do them for less, but you get less. The bars will blend with your current windows. The doors are pricier, but you want them to match your current motif. You don't have a homeowners' association, per se, but you don't want to stick out like Fort Knox and upset your neighbors by making upgrades they don't agree with. I'd say do the windows, doors and alarm first. Then do the bushes. The neighbors will think you got new windows. The doors will surprise them, but you need them."

"Can I keep my bushes, but trim them back?"

"Let's see," Hugh said.

Hugh and Kim walked outside, with Zach trailing. Hugh nodded. "You can. But we need to get that done today."

"What's the rush?"

"We've discovered a couple people we want you to take a look at."

"That's good." Kim turned to look at Zach, whose attention was on the sky.

"Come inside," he said. "That helicopter has flown by three times. I don't like it."

Kim did as she was told, flustered and unnerved by the seriousness of the Hood team.

Chapter 4

Kim paced her bedroom on the early Tuesday morning, swallowing Zach's words. *I always get my man or woman.* Did he really? Who was he? All the superheroes wrapped into one incredibly fit body?

Twenty-four hours had passed and nothing had happened. What if nothing happened at all? What if the attempts to kill her stopped altogether? Would he think she'd made things up despite their conversation yesterday? No. Nobody in their right mind would call her a liar. He'd seen the proof. He'd found it himself.

What was he doing now? Walking to the window, Kim parted the soft silk curtains and spotted Zach patrolling the west end of her property as he'd done all night long, looking like some crazed black ninja. The other Hoods had vanished last night as quickly as they'd appeared. Kim wanted to giggle, but the practical side of her recognized that Zach was suffering through the intense September Georgia heat for her benefit.

She'd had conflicting thoughts on hiring Hood Investigations in the first place. But who else would do what he was doing? At the moment, she had the note and the attack at the ice cream store, but she suspected the police chief would make light of those things. Zach had found the windows in the keeping room. A good lawyer could argue that she'd arranged that also. In a business where credibility was everything, hers could be on the line. Why did Zach believe her?

She'd given him twenty thousand reasons to believe her and to stay on her case. But this was about more than money. Hood Investigations as a corporation was extremely solvent, so in the scheme of things, twenty thousand dollars was of little consequence.

Zachary Hood *believed* her.

Somewhat relieved, Kim turned away from the window when the glass behind her exploded. Instinct took her to the floor as glass showered around her, splintering into her hair. She crawled under her four-poster bed, scared.

For ten agonizing minutes she waited, wishing she'd followed the plan she and Zach had discussed. If anything happened, she was to get into the laundry room, bury herself beneath the dirty clothes and wait for him there. She debated crawling down the hall to the room now, but her hands were rooted to the wooden floor, and she couldn't move. Her body wouldn't obey.

Feet thundered on the stairs leading to her bedroom, and she wished she had more than the mace she'd hidden under the bed to defend herself. Reaching for it, Kim held her breath, knowing she'd be found, hoping her captor would be Zach, and not the person who wanted her dead.

Her two-hundred-pound bed frame began to rise off two of its four-poster legs. "Come out from under there."

"The laundry room is clear," she heard a man say as she crawled from beneath the bed.

Kim looked up and saw a different version of Zach standing above her. A paw of a hand reached down and pulled her up with no effort. "The threat has been neutralized. What's that?" he asked, referring to the canister in her hand.

"Defense spray. I keep it under the bed." The inept spray against his 9 mm looked ridiculous, but she didn't let it show on her face.

Another man, an identical twin to Ben Hood—Zach's brother—came into the room, looked at the canister, then at her. He looked a little apprehensive. "You have to have great aim with that, or it's no good. Rob Hood," he stated by way of introduction. "Ma'am. You were hit. Sit down."

"No, I wasn't." Two seconds passed, and she realized by his expression that he wouldn't lie to her. "Where?"

Ben and Rob never touched her, but they crowded her with their bodies until she backed into the bed. She had no choice but to sit down. Though she wasn't easily intimidated, they did a good job of making her feel small.

"Where am I hurt?" Looking down, she could see no injury.

The air seemed sucked dry when Zach entered the room. He practically tossed his brothers aside, getting to the bed. "Your cheek," he exhaled. He grabbed her hand before it could reach her face. "Don't touch it! Dammit, Ben, go in the bathroom and get the cotton balls and antiseptic. Rob, get outside with the cops. Hugh's out there already."

Zach cursed some more, his hands moving down her shoulders to her elbows. He looked under her arm, and feeling self-conscious at his lack of decency, she yanked her arm down.

"You hurt anywhere else?" he asked, not knowing why she'd reacted so abruptly. In some things men were so dense. She didn't want him looking at her armpit.

"No. I didn't know I was hit. I don't feel anything. It must have just grazed me. I—I do recall that, but everything was going so fast, honestly, I had no idea—"

His brother returned with the first aid kit, and they went to work in silence. Ben, with slow, careful hands, picking glass from her hair, and Zach dabbing and blowing lightly to soften the sting on her injured cheek where the bullet had grazed her.

Four focused, concerned eyes were studying her, and she couldn't help but become even more self-conscious. "I'm not accustomed to this much attention. I'm fine. Fellas, please." Kim squirmed off the bed, but Ben sat her down again.

"Be still. I'm not finished. Zach, we should call Xan.

I don't know how to get the rest of this glass out of her hair."

"Come on, Ben. Pick it out a piece at a time. I'll do it."

"No, man. I got it."

They were so patient with each other, Kim thought, her heart tender for what she'd missed out on as a child.

"Who's Xan?" Kim wanted to know.

"Our sister. She's a doctor," Zach answered. "I don't want anyone to know the judge has been hurt."

"She's done hair before," Ben said in his own defense. "I just don't want to hurt her."

"Just take your time, B," Zach said. "You're getting it out, but you should probably call anyway."

"Good idea," Ben said. "Let me see what she's doing."

"How'd I get shot?" Kim reached for her cheek, but Zach caught her hand and gently guided it down to her lap. He sectioned her hair and pulled fragments of glass from the strands.

"Your neighbor next door was shooting at the squirrels that were eating from his bird feeder, and he misfired when a squirrel ran at him."

"Paul shot me?" Incredulous, Kim ran to the window, but Zach didn't allow her to look out. "I need to talk to him. Has he lost his mind?" Paul, the retired dentist with bad teeth. Paul, who'd scratched his cornea with a piece of mail two months ago. Paul had shot her. She was going to kill him.

Angrily she headed to the hallway and had her

foot on the first step, when Zach caught her wrist and wouldn't let go.

"Where are you going?" he asked calmly.

"To have it out with him."

"We're taking care of that."

She looked between the two Hoods. "You're standing here with me, doing nothing. I'm trying to stop him from killing me, something you're obviously incapable of doing."

"You'd have been shot whether I was here or not. Lucky for you I was here."

Ben looked around, covered his mouth as he was leaving and coughed *stupid* into his hand. "I'm going outside to talk to Xan. Stressed," he said to Zach as he eyed Kim.

They were alone now, and Zach had backed her up to her bedroom doorway. "What's this really about, Kim? Are you stressed out?"

"I was shot!"

"You were grazed."

"It doesn't matter. Maybe he's the psycho who's been leaving me notes. Did you interrogate him?"

Zach shook his head. "He's not our guy."

Frustrated, Kim crossed her arms over her chest. "How do you know? You only met him for five minutes. He has a gun, and he's obviously got anger issues."

"I accused him of trying to kill you, and he wet his shorts."

Despite her frustration, her anger took a nosedive. She and Zach shared a moment of silence, and she tried hard to hide her smile. So did Zach.

"Yikes."

"Yeah," Zach said. "Not our man."

To keep her smile locked in, Kim curled her lips into her mouth. "Are the police already here?"

"Yeah. They arrived just as the, uh, urine ran from the bottom of his khaki shorts to the top of his knee-high tube socks."

She nodded. That was Paul's uniform. The seventy-eight-year-old man wore shorts even in the winter. He claimed he never got cold.

"What will happen to him?" Kim asked.

"We're going to dissect his life to be sure he doesn't have any crazy secrets, and then he'll be cited for firing a weapon without a permit." Zach no longer looked lethal or concerned. In fact, he looked disappointed. "You weren't in the laundry room as we discussed."

Kim shook her head. "I couldn't make it. I was scared. Like when I was a—I mean—I just couldn't get there."

His gaze raced over her. Not like she was a client, either. "Finish your sentence," he told her. "Like when?"

They were now at the top of the stairs. His brothers were still outside with the police, and he wasn't letting her slip of the tongue go. She'd never talked about her past to anyone. It was a secret for a reason, though no longer classified. But she liked to keep her past private.

She put on her judge's face for Zach. "I didn't make it because I was afraid. Getting under the bed was child-ish, so what is the big deal? It was Paul. Can I get some coffee now, please?"

"Zach, the police chief just arrived. He wants to talk to the judge. He's angry," Rob added from downstairs.

"Hold him for five minutes, then bring him into Kim's office."

"Let me check my face." In the mirror, Kim saw the bruise and knew it would get uglier before it would go away. She'd been lucky. Damn lucky. She did have a lot to thank Zach for. Her hair glittered with the slivers of glass from the window. Today's mishap would be an all day beauty correction she hadn't counted on. Again, she reminded herself she'd invited Hood Inc. into her life, and now she needed to cooperate in every way, including controlling her temper.

"Ready?" Zach asked, sticking his head into her dressing room.

A shiver raced over her. She still wasn't accustomed to having a man in her home, and in her life, but Zach was different in a more masculine, commanding way. She fanned her face, dabbed the wound that was only slightly swollen. "Yes, I'm ready."

The two headed down the stairs and Kim quickly got her coffee before sitting on her comfortable sofa.

"Kim, don't tell him too much."

"I don't know anything."

"You know why you chose us."

She shrugged and nodded. "His office wasn't taking my concerns seriously."

"Judge Thurman," Rob said from behind them to get their attention. "The police chief would like to ask you some questions."

The chief had just celebrated his fifty-ninth birthday,

his balding scalp ringed with what remained of his hair. He wasn't a blustery man, but he was persistent in a silent, intense way. He made her uncomfortable in his effort to intimidate, only because he annoyed her. She normally excused herself from his circle at cocktail parties, but today she was his focus.

She would make this quick and as pain free as possible. "What can I do for you, Chief Vorhees?"

"Why would you go with Hood and not a law abiding group like, oh, say, the cops?"

"Look here—" Zach started, when Kim reached over and squeezed his hand.

"Hood Investigations is a law abiding group, and they do what your officers didn't do, which is to believe me. I called your office Friday, the day my assistant and I were attacked and nearly kidnapped, and we were told that someone would take a report. Are you here to do that today?"

He had the audacity to look insulted. "Hardly."

"Exactly why I chose Hood. They get results. While your officers were on my detail, someone has been trying, and rather successfully, to break into my house—"

"That's not true."

Zach nearly spoke and Kim raised her hand a bit, keeping her voice low and controlled.

"—through my keeping room. And your officers, who have been on my security detail, have been sitting around with their thumbs up their asses, doing who knows what, as I'm about to be killed. Excuse me, Rob, for my bad language. But Chief, I've all but let the fox into the henhouse. Or are they the foxes?"

"I can assure you that they are not." He laughed uncomfortably. Alone. "I can guarantee your safety, Judge."

"Really? Even Hood couldn't promise me that."

The chief broke in. "You didn't give us a chance. I've done regular checks on my staff. I will personally investigate this new information about the break-in and the kidnapping." He waved his hand from side to side as if he didn't believe it had even happened. "All the changes you're having done outside are just cosmetic. They're unnecessary and they won't stop a determined criminal."

"That attitude is why I hired Hood. They value my life and my money. I asked for your help and you didn't take me seriously. You asked me to justify the increase in security and even though I gave you ample reasons, I was still denied. My life and my death would have been on your hands, and quite frankly, I'm unwilling to risk either."

"Judge Thurman, we just don't have the resources to assign extra personnel without a viable, confirmed threat. Those notes Hood showed me?" He shrugged them away. "Any child can leave a note on your gate. That doesn't mean your life is in danger. But Hood's security agents are nothing more than glorified bouncers. They get results, but they're gangsters."

None of the Hood team took the bait. Kim was impressed. "The operative phrase for me is, 'they get results.' Chief, why are you wasting my time?"

"Judge, I beg your pardon. To be honest, I'm insulted. We increased patrols in your neighborhood, and the officers know some of the children. We've done what we can do to help you."

"Then how was someone able to break into my home while your officers work here every day? And how was I nearly kidnapped and my assistant's arm broken, and you not take that attack seriously?"

He looked alarmed. "I did hear about that and we are looking into it. I can add a couple men to your detail, and Hood can be backup."

"So that when I'm dead, you can sound as if you did great things for me at my memorial? Thanks for stopping by. Rob, see the chief out."

The portly man stood, rolling his hat through his hand. "It looks bad. Like you don't have faith in the police department."

"How it looks isn't my problem."

She extended her hand to Zach, who helped her up. "I'm ready whenever you are."

"Let's get your hair done." Zach was a man she could definitely keep around.

The chief scoffed as he lumbered toward the door.

"Chief, while your men patrol the neighborhood, maybe they can keep an eye out for my attempted murderer before one of my pint-size neighbors becomes collateral damage."

The chief's head snapped up, but Kim breezed right by him and out the door.

Chapter 5

Kim's hair took four hours to complete.

Zach would rather have been anywhere else. The women in the shop wanted to know who he was and why he was there. When he finally escaped outside, he didn't go back in. It was arguably the longest four hours of his life.

When Kim finally emerged, she looked beautiful. The diamond studs in her ears sparkled as her hair swung fresh and clean, playing peekaboo with the glistening jewels.

"What?" she asked, looking over her shoulder. "You're staring."

"You're cute. Get in the car."

"That's supersweet." She laughed. "I'm sure your girlfriend is so happy." She shut her eyes and pretended to tremble. "I just feel the love."

"I don't have a girlfriend."

"Not if those are your lines. 'You're cute, get in the car.' So what's next on our list?"

"I can see why you don't have a man in your life. You run men over."

"What?" Kim stopped laughing. "What are you talking about?"

"You ran the chief's ass down like he was a scooter and you were the Ultimate Aero, one of the fastest, most expensive cars in the world."

"He deserved it." She puckered her lips and pulled down the visor in his truck to admire her hair. Her cheek was as puffy as it was going to get. She just hoped it didn't bruise too badly. Suddenly self-conscious, Kim closed her hands and tucked her chin. Sitting back, it occurred to her that he wasn't Clark. Zach was a different kind of man. He didn't bother to watch his words. He was very straightforward. "The chief thought he could sell me a bill of goods about why he wasn't doing his job and I wasn't buying it. Too bad he got told off. I was just being honest."

"You pulverized the man, and the thing is, we still might need him. Not only that, I have to wonder if that's why you're alone."

"So that's it? You see me angry once and this turns personal? I'm alone because I choose to be."

"That can't be true. You're too caring and too concerned. I've watched you in court and while you were at home. You know how to love. You choose not to."

His words stung. He'd promised to know her underwear color, but her heart? Why was he trying to analyze her romantic life? "That's not true. A few years ago, I was in love and engaged, but he didn't want to get married. He decided that the restrictions on judges were too extensive and he didn't want to live his life within those parameters. So he walked away."

"Wow, that's deep."

Kim shrugged. "I've accepted the conditions of my life. I chose the law and it chose me. So there's nothing to be sorry for. Where are we going?" she asked.

"Back to your house to oversee the renovations. Then we follow the regular routine. You have to be exposed to some degree so the person takes the bait."

"I'm the bait?"

His half nod, half shrug said it all. "Unfortunately. I want you to have your cheek looked at."

"No, I'm fine. It's a bullet brush burn. I've had worse falling off a swing."

"Kim, does everything have to be your way?"

"No."

"Then why is it every time I tell you something you argue?"

"I don't, Zach. I simply don't think I need to see a doctor."

"You didn't want the suggested upgrades. You didn't want to listen when I told you not to confront your neighbor—"

At her gate, he put the truck in Park.

"But I did."

"After I had to stop what I was doing to explain everything to you. You're not trusting me. You're acting like you're six and I have to run everything by you. If you can do this yourself, then fire me. Otherwise, listen. Stop arguing. Let me do my job, so I can save your life. What's it going to be?"

No one ever talked to her this way. Not twice.

"I have more important things to do than babysit."

"Giving up control is very difficult for me. I thought I was doing a good job."

"I'll tell you what. You think about it. If you can't give up everything to me, then I can't help you."

He got out and opened her door and then the electric gate.

Kim walked in and turned when she felt him slide something into her hand. The gate remote. "Kim, you decide how you want things to play out. Call me tomorrow with your decision."

Zach whistled and caught his cousin Hugh's attention. He used sign language, and all construction stopped, and trucks were mobilized and driven off the property.

Zach slipped through the open gate, backed up his truck and drove away.

Everybody was always leaving. The irrational fear hit Kim like a hunger she couldn't feed. She walked up the driveway. Zach, Hugh, and all the contractors and crew were gone. The helicopter flew low, startling her.

Why was it there? It was something she'd never paid much attention to before, but because Zach had called it to her awareness, it was now an ever present and annoying reminder of her vulnerability and danger. Maybe this was Howard's, the last guy she'd somewhat dated, way of getting back at her. When she'd found him going through her work briefcase with his tiny camera, she'd dumped him. He'd been calling once a month for the past three months, and maybe now he'd amped up his game. He was a TV tabloid reporter for the local entertainment news network, and he probably needed a big scoop to keep his job.

Kim casually walked into the house and retrieved her putter and golf balls. Being a boarding school brat, she'd had her fill of dignified sports; golf being among them. She'd become quite good, but her mother had made it clear that no daughter of hers was going to pretend to make a living off a ball. So Kim had done the logical thing and made her living off lives, like her mom. She used a ball for recreation.

Kim lined up ten balls and adopted her stance as the copter hovered. So they *were* there to watch her. Hmm. The lesson began.

She balanced her club, adjusted her arms, pulled her arms back, pivoted and swung. The ball went right toward the windshield of the copter. There was no way she'd hit it. They were over the open field by the lake, but she was going to send a message for them to leave her the hell alone.

The pilot knew what was about to happen and pulled up. In quick succession, Kim hit the balls straight at the hovering vehicle. Frantic, the copter scrambled, jerking in the sky to get out of her firing line. She'd intentionally made her shots too short, but she kept swinging.

The cameraman was no longer filming, she noticed, but they had cleared her airspace and had ascended to a higher level. Good. They'd gotten the message. She wasn't in the mood for any more masculine nonsense. First the Baxters, then Zach Hood, then the chief and now the helicopter reporter. Enough was damn enough.

From the Sugarbakers' driveway, Zachary watched the judge pitch golf balls at the helicopter and didn't hide his laughter.

"She's pissed off," Ben murmured, watching, too. "Why are they filming her?"

"I was able to find out that it might be a magazine that wants to expose judges who don't work enough, but get paid full-time by taxpayers."

Rob Hood—Zach's oldest brother, Ben's twin and the president of Hood Investigations Incorporated—scoffed, as one who had recently earned his law degree and aspired to one day become a judge. "People need to understand how much work is involved. She works full-time. Hugh, what does her background check say?"

"Unlike anyone else we've ever checked out, everything she's told us is one hundred percent factual. Down to the exact dates and months. The judge is legit. Her parents are something else, though. Their entire life is blacked out. Also, her life from the years fourteen to eighteen are a blur."

Hugh was the computer geek of the family and the one cousin who had been taken into their home when his mother had passed away when he was fourteen. Hugh's father couldn't raise a son alone, and their fathers had been brothers. Hugh had fit in with the Hood boys since he was a toddler, and they'd only separated to go to college. He'd worked at the Pentagon and for the FBI, but now split his time between the government and Hood Inc.

Older than Zach by six months, Hugh was the quietest Hood, but he was brilliant in his own way. "Her family is intriguing," Hugh went on, typing on his computer. "It's almost as if they don't exist, but we know they do. I'm going to keep researching."

"She was in boarding school," Zach informed them. "She said she *visited* her parents."

Ben shook his head distastefully. "I would never do that to my kids."

"You would do what you have to for your future kids," Rob corrected him. "*Our* future kids," he said quietly. "Even if they are as bad as we were," he said, drawing laughs from his siblings and cousin. "But who sends their kids to boarding school?"

Hugh flipped open a folder on his computer and started typing. He swore softly. "She went to school in Switzerland. Very expensive and very exclusive. Most Americans don't have knowledge of this school, or the money needed to educate one's child there," he added.

"What did her folks do, Zach?" Rob asked, turning in his seat to look at his brother.

Zach shook his head. "I have no idea. She won't say. There's a room in the house that's called the 'keeping room.' It's decorated like in the old days. Heavy furniture, old-style velvet curtains. Kim said it was her mother's favorite room, but it's cold, and definitely no place a little girl would want to play."

"If her mother was in there, she'd want to be there," Ben informed him.

"But Kim didn't seem to have been close to her mother. She seemed like she wanted to escape the room. Like she wanted to run out of there."

"That only makes her more understandable. Her past is a big mystery. Her parents worked for the government," Hugh told them. "But her file has been black-marked. At eighteen she resurfaced and went to Yale for college, then law school. From then on her life has been an open book."

Ben cringed. "What'd they do to her?"

"Insulated her," Rob said quietly. "This sounds like they protected her from whatever they did for work. They were possibly trying to keep her safe. Who knows? Now we have to protect her."

Kim had walked back into the house and was now staring out the door, calling Zach on the phone. He looked at his phone screen, but didn't answer.

He played the voice mail for them to hear.

"It's Judge Thurman. Kim. I apologize for losing my temper with you earlier. I was referring to something from when I was a child. Definitely nothing relevant to my adult life. I really do need your help. Please come back. I will be more cooperative. I promise. Thank you."

The helicopter returned. Kim walked back outside with her golf club in hand, setting the phone on the step. She was one of the few people he knew who still had a home phone.

"Bet you five dollars she pitches one straight at the windshield," Rob said, digging in his pocket.

Ben didn't bother to reach for his money. "Too easy. She's going to knock the hell out of them this time. The last time she warned them and they backed off. This time she's going for the jugular."

Rob shook his head, adjusting his binoculars. "That fool has a camera. She won't do it. She's a sitting judge. She can't knock him out of the sky. She doesn't want to lose her job."

Kim started swinging the club like it was a baseball bat. She pointed at the copter, then played a little badminton with the golf ball and putter. She looked like she was having fun, too, until she batted the ball high as if it was a tennis ball, drew back and knocked the hell out of it.

The pilot didn't stick around to see if the ball was coming for him. He cleared the airspace above her house.

The men leaned forward, all four of them laughing. The ball landed somewhere deep in the field, where all the other balls had landed.

"She's got Hood in her blood. You sure you haven't tapped that already?" Hugh teased.

"Hell nah, man." Zach laughed deep and long. "She's all fire, all the time. I need my downtime. Kim doesn't know how to relax."

"Tame the savage in her," Rob advised. "LaKota was the same way. Wound up, angry, ready to fight all the time. I had to convince her I would protect her." Rob pulled out a photo of his exotic-looking wife and smiled. "I still feel like the luckiest man alive to have married her."

"I don't know why. LaKota's *still* wound up," Zach told him drily. "She damn near scratched my eyes out on Halloween."

"I told you not to come over in that dumbass werewolf costume. Something about that stupid costume scared her. You deserved exactly what you got."

"She tried to scratch my eyes out."

"You can see, so I think you're all right," Rob told him.

"Anything on who attacked her and Clark at the ice cream store?" Zach asked.

Ben nodded. "The license plate came back to one of the deputies' wives. Now she drives the SUV all the time, but Ice talked to her today and found out that on the day in question, the deputy said he needed to use the truck for surveillance."

"Why would the chief cover for him?" Rob asked.

"Because he's not really investigating. Asking your men—did you know anything about this?—as opposed to really investigating are two different things."

"Why was the wife so honest with Ice?" Rob asked Ben.

"Because she wants out of the marriage."

Zach watched Hugh open another folder on his computer. "What's this man's name?"

"Lieutenant Franklin," Ben said. "She said she's not leaving because he's cheating, but because he's been giving her money to this woman."

Zach's brothers froze for a moment, then agreed the lieutenant was indeed crazy and lucky to still be alive.

"Let's sit on the lieutenant for a minute and see where he leads," Rob said.

"No," Zach said. "We shook the trees and this is the result. I vote we move on this now."

"Hold, Zach," Ben told him. "We can't move too soon. Let's see what else might be happening with the lieutenant. Don't worry, we're going to get him."

Zach leaned forward, peering out the windshield. "Two days and then we take him down."

Rob, the president of Hood Inc., nodded. "Agreed."

With her golf club on the ground, Kim listened, and when she heard no more aerial disturbances, she walked around her yard gathering the scattered golf balls. Then she grabbed an automatic golf ball scooper and left her gate open as she scooped up errant golf balls.

Zach rolled his eyes. "Why do I have rules if she isn't going to follow them?" He opened the door on the truck and got out. "I'll check in later."

"Hey!" Ben called out and Zach stuck his head back inside the truck.

"What?"

"I bet she doesn't let you hold her scooper."

Zach told them all where they could go and slammed the door on their laughter. He caught up to Kim, who was sucking up golf balls, when his brother's truck rolled by. He took the scooper for a few seconds, knowing they were laughing at him.

"That's okay." Kim reached to take it back. "I can do it."

"I know you can."

Guilty eyes squinted at him. "I did something very bad, and I know it's probably going to be on the news."

"What did you do?"

"I hit a helicopter with my golf balls."

"What's a nice lady like you doing, acting like you don't have any sense?"

She stabbed at golf balls that littered the ground around the trees, scooping them into the scooper. "I administer the law, but I don't always have the law in me."

"Well, I'll be damned. You're a badass."

Kim cut her eyes at him, her smile small and sexy. She sucked up two golf balls and kept walking. "You fancy, huh," she rapped softly, catching Zach by surprise. He nearly tripped on the golf ball he'd bent down to pick up.

She gave him her best innocent face.

"Who are you, lady? You ain't nobody's judge that I ever met before. You rap, you have a tongue like a laser, you play golf like a pro *and* you're gorgeous."

"Don't flatter me. I might get used to it."

"There's no reason why you shouldn't. You're a beautiful woman. You should hear that all the time."

It was as if she didn't hear him anymore, the way she dipped into a cut between the trees that fit them single file. She wasn't worried about her newly done hair or her status. She hurried ahead, unafraid. She was beautiful, and she knew it. Why couldn't she hear it aloud?

"Kim, where are you going?"

"To a secret place. Come on," she whispered. The tall cedar trees blocked the sun, casting them into a false world of darkness. Kim took only a few seconds to stow the golf ball catcher and putter, then pushed forward deeper into the woods.

Her adventurous spirit challenged him, and Zach followed her. She made turns by memory. They must have walked a half mile, when he could hear water. "Where are we?"

"Almost there."

The summer heat hadn't bothered him, until now. He was climbing rocks and scrambling after a woman with a beautiful body. Zach finally caught her hand. "Where are we?"

"My favorite place. If you ever need to find me, I'll be here."

They broke through some woods and stood in a fine mist of water near a lake. "Is this the Chattahoochee?"

"I wish. It's a man-made lake to look like the Hooch. It's been here fifty years, and I love it. I had this friend, Carter, and her mother would pick me up for Girl Scouts, and we'd camp here when I was about seven."

Kim sat down and closed her eyes. Birds soared overhead, as the water flowed by. Kids in tubes kicked their feet and laughed, but Kim ignored them, seeking her own inner peace.

"Where's Carter now?"

"I don't know."

"You ever thought of looking for her?"

Her eyes were still closed and she shrugged. "No."

"Are you ever lonely?"

Her shrug was slower. "No."

"That's a lie."

"Are you my friend whisperer, Zach? Because I don't need that. Don't try to fix me. I'm not broken, okay?"

He'd never been so pleasantly put in his place. "Fair enough."

Kim pushed herself to her feet. "I've had enough sun for one day. I'll behave. Do as I'm told. I'll try not to argue. Are we good?"

Zach felt his mouth pull down. Everything she'd said was a lie. Her eyes and body language said so, but he'd try to work with her if she put forth a little effort. "We're good." He reminded himself he was always on the clock. "Yes."

"Have you come up with any leads?"

Zach kept his gaze forward. "Yes. In forty-eight hours, we'll have completed the review on your case."

"Sounds good. I'm anxious to get my life back."

Kim saw the helicopter in the distance and a dark look replaced her serious expression. "Let's go before they get a fix on me. That could be the person, for all I know."

She drew closer to Zach, and he understood, but wondered why someone would be stalking the judge from the sky. While she slept, he would find out.

Chapter 6

Kim sat through the motions portion of the trial, where the defense and prosecuting attorneys presented questions as to which evidence they would be allowed to present to the court. This would likely be one of the largest drug cases in Georgia's history, and Kim didn't want it screwed up because one of the attorneys decided to slip something in at the last minute.

This case would be by the book, and it would be held in Fulton County, Georgia, where the crime took place.

Waverly Phinney, the lead attorney for the defense, was from Philadelphia, and he used his intelligence and skill to slide through slippery doors that weren't always legally propped open.

The Committee for Ethical Standards had investigated him several times, but he'd always managed to slither behind the right case law and avoid punishment, but not down here in Georgia.

Kim wasn't having any of his nonsense.

He spoke quickly, hoping no one caught the undercurrent of his parenthetical put-downs, which were couched between shouted words and smiles.

Kim prided herself on her perfect hearing, even if her once-perfect vision had begun to betray her. She had six pairs of reading glasses. A pair always arm's length away. Two pairs were on her bench right now. She read the motion before her, then removed her glasses. Nevin Stuckey, the prosecutor, moved toward the bench, the defense attorney, Phinney, approaching also.

With the swiftness of a panther, Zach moved, and the attorneys stopped short. Each had been advised as to how to proceed to the bench. Any deviation would result in having to deal with Mr. Hood or the case would end in a mistrial. Neither wanted that. They each believed they would prevail.

Zach was dressed in a tailored black suit, his gun unmistakable beneath the jacket, and his tieless white collared shirt was crisp and bright. Kim's thoughts had become unrealistic for a few seconds as she daydreamed about sticking her nose in between his collar and his neck, and biting him softly. Blinking, she made the thoughts fly away.

Over the years, she'd had these thoughts from time to time, and normally would allow the flights of fancy. Fantasizing was as close as she would ever get to an affair. The Hood agents that were in the room, interspersed with her deputies, performed a synchronized rotation. Everyone was serious and quiet. Nobody looked happy. Zach had announced at the morning meeting three days ago that he was taking their lives apart as part of an intense investigation.

He believed in full disclosure; he also believed in psychological torture. He was making them sweat. His tactics were working. Two of the deputies had already called in sick.

Those that had come in were sweating. But nothing had happened. No one had tried to kill her. In a ridiculous way, Kim was almost disappointed. But Zach hadn't left her side in four days. Four days of nothing happening, besides her neighbor wetting himself from being scared by her security agent. That's what twenty thousand dollars had bought her. Pee.

Kim focused her attention on Phinney, who for someone in his young thirties was still cocky. He was a brilliant litigator who hadn't suffered enough of life's tribulations to know humility if it came up and bit him.

The prosecutor, though, had been around, and knew enough not to tip his hand. The case would be interesting, Kim knew. She just needed to focus.

"This motion is to suppress the wiretap evidence. It's all hearsay." Phinney smiled at her, saying, "Any idiot can see that. My client's name was mentioned in a call, and that's how we got here. That doesn't mean he was a drug kingpin."

"One thousand dollar fine for contempt. And the motion to suppress the wiretap is denied. Next?" Kim said.

Phinney looked at Stuckey, who kept his mouth shut. "Fine for what?"

"I would tread carefully, before you miss your client's trial for sitting in jail yourself, Mr. Phinney. The subject of idiocy had better not *ever* be brought up to me again. Step back."

He smiled coyly. "Ma'am, you simply misunderstood me. I was stating that this motion is so simple, any idiot could see that there is no direct evidence connecting my client to all other evidence of this case. This was a discussion on the telephone that was overheard about other people being investigated by the DEA. People can say they know a famous actor, but do not. That's what I referring to. But I'm sure you will agree with me that this is all a misunderstanding."

"The motion is still denied. The client was subsequently investigated and a case built separate and apart from that initial investigation. We call that evidence. Down here in Atlanta, we members of the court take offense to being called idiots, whether you intended to or not. Pay your fine of now *two thousand dollars*. I *got* your meaning, and I *don't* agree with you."

He started to speak, then thought better of it.

"That's right, Mr. Phinney. I didn't miss it that second time, either. The next contempt charge will include three days in jail and a five thousand dollar fine. Are we now understood?"

"Yes, Judge."

"See the clerk before you leave the courtroom."

His smile had lost some of its shine, but two grand wouldn't hurt him. This also wouldn't be the last time they butted heads.

He nodded and stepped back.

"Next motion?" Kim asked, noting the early evening hour. She'd get through the rest of the motions if it took all night.

Prosecutor Stuckey raised his hand, half standing. "Your Honor?"

"Yes?"

"I broke the crown on my tooth yesterday, and while I wouldn't ordinarily interrupt court and ask to go to the dentist, this trial may take weeks. I would like to not be a distraction later on."

Kim nodded. "What time is your appointment?"

"Fifteen minutes ago," he said quietly.

Kim licked the inside of her top lip. It was five-fifteen. Quitting time for normal people. So much for working late.

"Of course. Court will reconvene tomorrow morning at eleven o'clock." The prosecutor looked immensely relieved. He would at least get some rest tonight. "Dismissed."

Kim rose and left the bench. Zach had always been where she could see him. In her direct line of sight or in her peripheral vision. But when she stood and turned around, he was behind her. His brothers were twins, but she couldn't be sure that he wasn't a twin also. How could one man be in so many places at one time?

Zach's hands were sure as he helped her out of the courtroom. They moved in unison, but not toward her office. "Where are we going?"

"We're going to deviate from your routine today. Your office is temporarily down here now."

Zach opened double black doors that had been

marked Under Construction for the past three months. Kim had known new offices were being built, but nothing more. She had no idea how Zach had worked out her getting a new office. Or when he'd had the time to make any such deal. He'd always been with her. She gripped his hand, the light from the hallway growing dim as they edged inside. "Last week you said we had to stick to the routine and now we're deviating. What happened? Why is it dark in here?"

"We're in the very interior of the courthouse. There are no windows. You're safe here. There are several escape routes, also."

"I'm already safer with you. Tell me what happened. You promised me an update a couple days ago, and you still haven't given it to me."

"You're right. Let's sit down and talk."

His grip on her hand tightened a bit, and he guided her up and past him. "Lights on," he said quietly, and the lights brightened the room. A desk similar to hers had been placed in the room. While the office wasn't exactly like hers, it was close enough. The effort was commendable and would help ease some of the concerns for her safety.

"Everything is voice activated." He put a remote in her hand. "To program, say 'doors lock.'"

Kim repeated the words and the doors locked. He showed her how to call for emergency services and how to call him directly. The technology was sophisticated and sleek.

Even after the long day, Kim wasn't ready to go home. She sat down and stretched.

"How did you get all this accomplished?" she asked him.

"Hugh was instrumental in getting the technology up and working. I'm waiting for him to come in so we can give you that update I promised you last week about your case. Are you hungry? You didn't eat a lot at breakfast." Zach watched her closely.

"I'm not hungry." Even as Kim denied it, her stomach rumbled in protest.

"Your body is telling on you." He walked to the small kitchen off the office and returned with hummus and vegetable crackers.

Kim looked in his hands. "Who's that for?" She crossed her legs, stroking them.

"You," he said, laughing. "At home, your refrigerator is full of this stuff."

"I don't want hummus. I want meat."

"All right," he said, as if seeing her for the first time. After so many hours on the bench, he knew she needed some downtime. "Don't get indignant. A second ago you weren't hungry at all." He teasingly shook the hummus in her direction. Kim turned her arm away and frowned.

"I was fine until you broke out the vegetable crackers. I'm a real woman who needs real food, mister."

Kim pulled the pins from her hair and ran her fingers through it, releasing the tension of the day as she stroked the long, curly strands. She moved her shoulders and stretched her neck muscles. Eyeing a door with handles, she walked over. "Closet?"

He nodded.

She kicked off her heels, and let her feet sink into

the brand-new carpeting. "Where are we eating, Mr. Hood?" She stretched and pulled her muscles in slow motion. He heard little pops and small moans. Bending forward, she let her body drop, her fingers reaching for her toes.

Zach watched her closely. "What are you hungry for?"

"Anything. Put me on a boat, and I'll go fishing for my own food." For a woman who'd been in a chair for hours, she was amazingly limber. Holding her ankles, she rocked her hips side to side, then stepped shoulder length apart. Linking her hands behind her back, she lifted her arms, and he heard two loud pops. Finally, she dropped her hands and wiggled.

He threw his head back and laughed.

Turning her head, she looked at him. "What, Zachary?"

"I'm Zachary now? Fine. What are you doing?"

"Releasing tension and letting the blood flow to my brain."

"Feel better?" he asked. His eyes reflected interest.

"Much." He felt it, too. That flow of sexually tense energy that had captured her attention within hours of their meeting. She'd been ignoring it for days, but today, she felt vulnerable in his presence. Like she could yield to her womanly needs. Those long-forgotten needs that she'd been so adept at putting aside. They'd been together a week, but she'd been thinking back to their initial meeting two years ago and then six months ago.

Each time, she'd kept her eyes on him, watching his every move. Wishing she knew more about the man in black. He'd looked dangerous at times. Imposing against his detainees. He'd needed no introduction when his detainees were brought before her. When other deputies and marshals had struggled with inmates, the Hoods never had. They never raised their voices, and they never abused the men and women they were in charge of capturing.

In the self-defense classes, it was a whole different story. She'd been in Zach's arms several times. So had fifty other female judges, but that hadn't mattered. He'd taught them about kicking their way out of trouble, flipping and throwing a man, and disabling an assailant in order to get away. She could give a man a bloody nose because of Zach.

The way he held her now was much different, though. When her hand was within his, she was his only focus. His biceps against her was a delicious feeling. She couldn't help herself. She felt very womanly next to him.

Maybe he would be interested in playing with her. She searched for the perfect words…for the perfect moment to ask him to not only save her life but to be her—well, not her perfect lover. That sounded demeaning. He made more money than her; he certainly didn't need her.

Maybe they could be each other's perfect affair. No strings. They had their own public lives and too much to lose to be silly, jealous, crazy people when it was over.

With her hair hanging down and her butt in the air,

she saw through the mirror in Zach's eyes what she never saw in Clark's.

Attraction.

Kim stood up and her cheeks were flushed. The bruise from last week's incident had been covered up by makeup, and now that her energy was back, she felt new again.

Her head throbbed and so did her womanhood. "I'm starving now," she said.

"Are we still talking about fishing?"

Kim went over to the mirrored wall next to him to scrunch her mess of curls and line her lips. Inside the lines, she swabbed clear red gloss that made her lips look good enough to lick clean. "I can fish. Don't let the designer dress fool you."

"Look here, prep school. Those hands haven't touched fish guts. I don't believe that for one second."

Draping her pashmina over her shoulders, Kim didn't bother to defend herself.

Zach had her hand before she could stop him, and the full blossom of connection she'd been thinking of happened right then. She was in front of him in a second, their worlds meeting, their lives merging.

"Do you believe in honesty, Zach?"

"Only when it serves the right purpose." He was being honest now. There were no barriers between them.

"May I be honest?"

He traced the unbroken line on her hand that extended to the pulse on her wrist, and he pressed.

"There's a risk in telling me the truth." Her pulse raced against his fingers.

"I'm accustomed to my limitations."

"You're not the only one involved, Kim."

"You and I share an enviable, common quality. Self-control." He was still pressing against her pulse, her truth meter. He wanted to know how much she'd invest in what may come of them.

"You're stubborn and argumentative and you challenge me, Kim."

"I make you think, Zach."

"Kim, you want to tell me about this intense feeling between us. Then I'm going to have to decide what to do about it. If I can stay on this case or not."

"You're not going anywhere."

"How do you know?"

"Because you're invested in my case and in me. You finish what you start. Whatever happens between us personally, you won't walk away professionally. You have too much integrity and character for that. That's what I like so much about you. Being attracted to you is an added benefit."

His smile was quick. "I would be crazy to touch you. For thinking this perfect moment could extend beyond that door."

"It can't, can it?" Something good was slipping away. Kim felt it.

He shook his head.

Her fingers curled around his, growing to know the hand that was becoming as familiar to her as her own. She held his every day.

His close examination brought to her attention how sensitive her fingers were. How she loved to have them stroked and, in the best of situations, kissed. How she loved having them massaged.

He noticed her manicure, the soft pink polish and the butterfly ring she wore on her right hand. "What changed you?" he asked. "Two days ago you were fighting against me."

"I realized you had my back. Even if nothing was happening. Every second of every day you're with me. I could fight or get along. I choose the latter. But I understand if nothing can happen between us." Kim eased her hand away.

"I'm glad you understand. You feel like Italian?" he asked.

"Thai," she suggested. "I'd like something hot and spicy."

His eyes narrowed. "You are," he said.

"Excuse me?"

"Hot and spicy, Judge. But that's a subject for another time. Ready to go?" he asked.

She'd opened the door and he'd closed it.

There was a commotion beyond the door, and Zach was pulled out of their gentle flirtation. His gaze turned hard, and she remembered why they were there.

He released her hand, and the connection between them was like vapor in a suddenly ventilated room. Kim always forgot how massive he was until he put her behind him. With his gun drawn, he moved her quietly to a small enclosure in the wall—a small room, she realized—and told her to stay there in the dark. Then Zach was gone.

Minutes passed, and Kim had no idea what was going on, but she waited, worried about herself and Zach and the rest of the agents. Who was trying to hurt her? Who wanted her dead?

The room she was in was no larger than a dressing room, and had a small bench inside. So she sat, her legs crossed, her purse on her lap. She dug inside, happy when she found her defense spray. Palming it, she waited, her mind racing, praying Zach would come back.

How had her mother and father done this for so many years? Sat in small places, listening to other people's secrets? How could they stand being away from her? She hated being alone, but she'd resigned herself to accepting the fact that this was her life. Life had been dealt to her from this deck of cards.

She wore Wang, Mizrahi and Louboutin. Had Roth IRA accounts, investments and savings. She owned real estate, belonged to the right associations and had achieved great accomplishments in her career. She was successful.

Kim waited as the quiet closed in around her. If someone killed her right now, who would miss her? A tear trickled down her cheek.

The door was pulled open, and Kim jumped up, defense spray out and ready. Her hand shook slightly, but she was sure she would hit her target. "Who are you?" she asked.

"Zachary," he said, easing her arm down. As soon as he touched her she knew it was him. Her arm gave out.

"What happened? Is Hugh okay? He never showed up."

"He's fine. Bomb threat in the parking deck on Mitchell Street. We're moving now."

She turned her face away from Zach, and dabbed her cheek to be sure the wetness was gone. "Are we okay? Can we get out?" She heard her words and hated being that nervous, scared female. She closed her lips so no more inane words would flow out.

He hustled her through a door into a room with no air-conditioning.

"We're good. Why are you crying?"

"I'm not. I need my flats in case we have to run."

Zach pulled them from the back of his waistband. "Right here. Take my hand and don't let go."

Her hand firmly in his, Kim didn't stop running until Zach did.

Chapter 7

The restaurant was quaint, but Zach wasn't a fan of food with the head, legs and tentacles still on. "It's a shrimp!" Kim insisted.

He shrugged. "I don't care. I'm not eating it."

"It's already dead." She laughed at him. "Just cut that part off and eat it. You're being a baby about this."

"So? You can't punk me off, Kim," he told her. There were a lot of things he put into his mouth, but food that was staring at him wasn't one of them. "In fact, watching you maul the thing turns me off," he joked. "I'm not hungry anymore. I'll eat at my sister's house later."

"Who's the best cook in your family?" Kim drank tea while eating.

Zach ate his cabbage. "Now you're trying to get me killed."

Kim slipped a piece of shrimp onto his plate and he

ate it. "Why? It's a simple question. It could be one of your brothers."

"I'm not taking the bait. You're still a lawyer at heart, Your Honor, and I refuse to answer on the grounds that my words will get me starved to death at all future holiday dinners."

Kim gave him more of her shrimp and Zach ate without saying anything. He still hadn't gotten a handle on her yet. Though she was hungry, she was feeding him her food. There was this nurturing quality about her that reminded him of his sisters, but then again, he was attracted to Kim, and that hadn't happened before with a client.

"What's your favorite holiday food?" he asked.

She shook her head. "I don't eat anything special on holidays."

"Do you have a favorite holiday? Do you go anywhere? Do anything?"

Kim shook her head. "Not really. I like Easter. But now I rarely celebrate holidays beyond making sure my staff has them off, and that's pretty much Clark's job. Sometimes I travel. I went to Egypt last year. It was lovely."

"My favorite holiday is Christmas," Zach told her. "You've got to see my sister Xan's house at Christmas. She goes crazy. Lights everywhere, three trees lit up for the entire block to see. Santa on the rooftop, reindeer on the lawn, elves everywhere, music. The nativity scene is beautiful. She goes all out. She's nuts," he added almost as an afterthought.

Kim laughed. "Who sets all that up?"

"Who do you think? This year I'm going to be busy, because last year I was freezing my butt off, and she wouldn't help me! Claimed she had too much baking to do. Once the holiday is over, I have to pack everything up and take it all back to storage. In her defense, she cooks like our mother, so I give her the time she needs to throw down in the kitchen. I stay over there just to eat first. She does a little preholiday dinner. You know...I help her out," he said, sheepishly.

"You've got a disease. Seek help," she teased him.

Zach made eye contact with Kim and they burst out laughing. "Yeah...that sounded a little desperate, didn't it? I'm stalking my sister for her food. You've given me all your shrimp. Don't think I didn't notice."

Kim shrugged, enjoying the easy banter between them. "Mr. Fattel, the owner of this place, is very generous in his portions. I don't want to have leftovers. So, Xan is the best cook?"

"I will deny saying it, but yeah. Ben is great on the grill, now that he's married. Before, he was just all right. Hugh's a decent bartender until I show up, but unlike me he lacks imagination."

"How's that possible?" Kim didn't believe a word he was saying. "Drinks are like anything else. You follow recipes."

Zach shook his head. He was winding up and she could tell. She tried hard not to laugh at the big lie he was about to tell. "How did those drinks get invented? That's what I do. I like to invent new drinks. Sometimes I'm good. Sometimes, not so good."

"You suck," she tossed out there casually and drank her tea.

Shock lit up his face. "The hell you say, woman?"

"You're setting me up for the big lie. You're a terrible bartender." Kim laughed, sitting back in her chair, confident she'd read him right.

"Look here, Lady Law, just because you've got a badge doesn't mean you can cast disparaging remarks on my drinks." He could barely contain his laughter. "Which, by the way, you haven't tasted. I'm an excellent bartender. Except when things go bad. Then we've got problems, but that's rare."

"Aha!"

"Aha, nothing. I'm telling you, I've had a few mess ups. Who said furniture designers haven't had a few people slip off their couches?"

"You're not serious! You make people slip off couches or worse?" Kim laughed so hard, she covered her mouth. "What was your worst drink?"

Zach was the family clown. How did they deal with him? Her life didn't feel at risk, and she didn't feel the terrible pressure that had been her constant companion since she'd come to the realization that someone was trying to kill her.

"This conversation has stayed positive," he said, looking around as if he needed to escape. "Let's keep it that way."

"Come on. We're friends now." At his raised eyebrow, she corrected herself. "We're mortal enemies." His expression didn't change. "You own me until you find my nutcase."

"I like that. Cayenne and strawberry daiquiri."

Kim froze, her mouth slightly open. "You couldn't possibly have thought that would make a good drink."

"You thought shrimp with the eyes was good, so I know you're not talking."

Kim wiped her mouth and closed it. "I'll have you know that's a delicacy in a foreign country or somewhere."

"I can make that daiquiri into a good drink. Something is missing, but I'll figure it out."

He had a smile so slow and sexy growing on his face, she wanted to reach out and trace it. "Good sense is what's missing."

"I'm hurt that you're criticizing me."

"You'll make it. Who's left? What about your oldest brother, Rob?"

"Rob's the best at everything."

"Now, that's love."

He shrugged. "What can I say? Rob's the man. I'm the taster. That's my job and nobody is better at it than me."

Kim shook her head. "Are you the baby in your family?" Zach nodded. "How old are you?" she asked.

"Thirty-two. And you?"

"You know everything about me. I'm thirty-four. I bet you're good at being the baby in the family."

"Hey…hey. Don't turn this into something negative," he teased. "My job is important, and I do it well. Everybody knows their roles. I'm the man they go to when they need something done."

"I see. Did you finish college?"

Zach hated this turn in the conversation. Women usually liked him until this very moment. But he never shied away from who he really was. "No, I didn't finish. I didn't need a degree in geology to understand human nature."

"But don't you think a couple should be matched evenly with regard to education and economics?" she asked.

"In some instances, but not always. Your logic explains why there are so many single brothers."

Kim's neck snapped back. "I disagree. There are far more single women than there are men."

"That might be true. Women have outpaced men in education. If your philosophy holds true, your women friends are never going to get a man because a lot of men, good men, don't have BAs, MAs or PhD's. A lot of women like you won't give men like me a chance."

"I would, if I were looking, but I'm not." She sipped her tea and put the delicate cup back on the table. "How would a man combat that?"

"My life is very simple, Judge. I don't like what I can't have."

"And what you *can* have?" she asked.

"I like a lot," he finished for her. "It doesn't help that a lot of men are in jail. That lessens the dating pool for women."

"I hope that's not my fault," she told him, sipping her tea again.

"I can't blame you for doing your job."

"Thank you. You don't know how often I've heard

that it is my fault." Kim sighed and looked around. "I think I'm ready. Are you?"

"Just about. I wanted to tell you who we think is after you. Lieutenant Franklin. He's had access to your house and your chambers. His wife's SUV has some of the same license plate characters as the SUV used in the attempted kidnapping, and he was off work on the day of the attack. We're building a case against him."

"What's Hood going to do?"

"We're tailing him around the clock. He can't breathe and we not know about it. We don't want him to know that we're on to him. So when you see him at work, don't let on. Understand?"

Kim nodded. "Of course. Thank you. He really can't get to me?"

Zach shook his head. "Not without stopping by hell first."

Her neck snapped back. "Okay. Sounds good to me."

Silence floated around them and Kim wasn't sure what to do next. He'd just unloaded a lot of information on her, but she was grateful. It would take time to process, though. Grateful, she slid out of the booth. "I need to visit the ladies' room and then I'll be ready."

He walked her to the back, then scoped out the street through the storefront window as he waited for her.

Zach had finished eating a long time ago. He'd found the conversation revealing. Kim had tested the waters with him, and he wondered why. She didn't date. She didn't have family. Her curiosity was normal. Most clients wanted to know about the Hoods. They were an unusual bunch. But he had to be careful with her. She'd had a genuine interest in their family dynamics. He just hoped she knew that soon she'd return to her life and Zach to his.

While she was in the restroom, Zach stepped aside to get an update and apprise them of their next move.

Looking out the storefront window, he could see water shooting into the air and a crew working to get it under control. His team was around the corner, working their way toward him, but it would be another forty-five minutes. The streets were gridlocked.

"What's going on?" Kim asked.

"Water main break."

Kim pushed the door open to exit the restaurant. "Happens all the time. Want some ice cream? My favorite shop is right down the plaza."

Zach grabbed her arm and was surprised when Kim resisted. "Hey, wait," he said. "We work together. Let me first take care of the bill."

"I already paid."

"Kim, I'll take care of our bills."

"Okay, I'm sorry! I can't be wrong any more today," she said, exasperated.

Zach wouldn't let her go. "This isn't a man-woman thing. This is a tax thing. You're the client. If you pay for things while we're working, it's hard to explain at tax time. Do you understand?"

Put in her place, Kim turned her face away, and when she looked at him again, he could tell that she'd put her personal feelings aside. "Of course. My mistake. I feel like nothing significant, like I'm wasting your time.

Maybe I was just being paranoid. Can we go? I'm tired of being inside."

"You're not wasting my time. The person is probably aware that you have protection. They're probably assessing the risk of messing with you. If they're smart, they'll go away. Most times they're not. They get more cocky and want to try something else. This is going to sound crazy, but be patient."

They stepped outside and began walking toward the ice cream store.

Zach watched everyone and everything. Kim seemed less stressed now that she'd unburdened herself and was outside. Being closed up bothered him, too. That's why he hadn't gone back to finish college. He hadn't shared with Kim why he'd quit college in the final week of school. His mother had passed away, and being in the house that week had been hell. All he could think about was going from four years of stifling classrooms to the airless offices of corporate America.

There was no way he was going to spend the rest of his life in an office cube. Finishing his final exams had had no meaning after that. Zach had worn the rebel label well, but it only suited the purpose of not doing what was expected. He'd needed to get over missing his mom. She'd been his best friend. He'd recently received a letter from the school stating he had six months to take his finals. They'd left the door open for him. His mom would tell him to finish. He knew she would. He just needed to walk through the doors, but he hadn't found the motivation.

The evening sun had receded behind full white

clouds, the echoes of children playing down the plaza bounced up the sidewalk through the chatter of their parents. He wondered if Kim regretted not having a family of her own. She was still young. She could still have a family, but there was a lonely contentment to Kim he didn't understand.

"You have to get bored, Zach."

"Is that a question?" Their footsteps fell silent in unison.

"Don't you, though?"

"I never get tired. Each case is different. I travel, help others, and I change people's lives. How many people can say that?"

Kim's eyes were magnetic in that when she looked at him, there was a strong force that pulled him into her gaze and locked them together. "I believe you should do what you love. If this is it, then you've won half the battle of life."

Inside the ice cream store, the line was long and wrapped once around a rope. Kim studied the menu, while Zach studied everyone inside. He checked on the position of the team. They were still thirty minutes away. The workers were busy behind the counter, while one swept and wiped down the tables in the sparse eating area.

Kim seemed more interested in what other customers were buying. She'd just eaten. How could she possibly want more food?

As she gazed longingly at an overflowing bowl of sweetness, he realized that this was her guilty pleasure. She allowed herself this one joy because she indulged in few others. While in court she never smiled. Never broke the strict composure of her position. Here, she was like everyone else.

When it was her turn, Zach half listened to her order, noting instead the comings and goings of the patrons. He faced the entrance, watching the interior of the shop. If someone was going to make their move, it would be here. They were exposed.

At the register, Kim pulled out her wallet, then put it away.

"For here," she told the clerk as Zach handed over a twenty dollar bill.

"Keep the change and bag it, please. We have to go," Zach told Kim.

"Let's eat here. I got you one, too," Kim told him. "Please," she pleaded. "We're going to be in the rest of the evening."

The clerk, Keon, just stood there with the money in his hand. "We have that table in the corner that you like," he pointed out to Kim. "Either way, do I still get to keep the money?"

Kim's eyes begged Zach, and he wondered why mountains weren't moved by her silent plea. He gave in. "We can stay only until the team arrives. Then we leave."

"Okay." Her smile was quick and heart melting. So much pleasure for something so small.

"I'll bring it out to you after it's made," Keon said, cheerfully shoving his hefty tip into his pocket.

"We're out of vanilla," the manager said.

"Got it," Keon said and headed toward the back.

Kim sat down, while Zach stood by the door, watching everyone who walked by.

The sundaes were delivered, but they weren't pretty and neat. They were spilling over the bowl. Still, Kim could feel her excitement at the sight of the treat. She didn't do this often. Ice cream was supposed to be fun. Using her spoon, she ran it around the rim of the bowl and scooped up the falling treat, sticking it into her mouth. The creamy delicacy was delicious.

"Can I have sprinkles?" Kim asked, noticing her favorite finish was missing.

The young man had turned so quickly she could barely catch him. "Excuse me. Keon, can you bring me some sprinkles?"

"Sure," he said over his shoulder. "Be right back."

Kim drew back, surprised. For a young man so happy to get a tip a few minutes ago, he was sure acting ungrateful now. "Keon, you made a mess," she said, but he was gone. Just as quickly, he disappeared into the back.

Looking for napkins, Kim ate another spoonful of her ice cream, then pushed the spoon deep into the sundae. It tasted a little odd. She definitely needed sprinkles and napkins.

Rising, she waited for several customers to pass, got the items herself, then went back to her seat. Once there, she was shocked to see that her sundae was a fizzling, bubbling mess that was eating into the laminate on the table. Suddenly her heart couldn't beat correctly. It skipped several beats, then pounded. She was in trouble. *Zach!*

A passing woman sniffed. "That smells like sulfuric acid. Was that your ice cream?"

"What's wrong with the ice cream?" a mom cried, causing a panic that rippled through the small restaurant.

Horror struck Kim in the gut. She'd put ice cream in her mouth. She turned, her arms outstretched for Zach, her mouth open. His arms encircled her waist and he pushed patrons out the door.

"I ate some. I ate some of it," she mumbled into his ear.

"It's going to be okay," Zach said calmly. "Don't panic. Step outside and stay against the wall while I call the police. Don't eat anything," he told a woman, as he eased her spoon away from her mouth.

The manager ran outside, checking on patrons, while an employee walked around with her cell phone, videotaping everyone. Everyone was checking each other's mouths, while children cried because their moms had taken away their treats. The crying increased the tension.

The heat had begun to wear off the September day, and a gusty breeze tossed dried leaves through the plaza. Kim covered her mouth and coughed, then slowly pulled her hand away. No blood.

"Open your mouth," Zach told her. Their torsos touched, and she was aware of the size of his entire body and how he was shielding her. He examined her teeth and tongue. He got very close to her. He held her face and felt all the way down her neck as he looked inside her mouth.

"Your teeth look fine and your tongue is still pink. How do you feel?"

"I don't know. Is anything bleeding? What about my cheeks? Did you look under my tongue? Tell me."

A lady started crying as blood seeped from the corner of her mouth. There were terrified screams, and once the parents erupted, children cried louder.

"Oh, my goodness, Zach. Don't be afraid to tell me." Kim was holding his arms at the back of his elbows. She couldn't read his expression, except to note that he looked concerned.

Her hands slid up to his neck and she started to hop. "Zach! Tell me. Oh, my God! Am I going to die?"

"Kim, stop!" She read pain in his eyes, but also fear. *He's lying to me.*

Her emotions zigzagged, and just as soon as she felt the click release on her ability to reason, Zach pressed his lips to hers. "Kimberly," he said softly. He kissed her again and again, calling her name. She trembled against his strength, yet he held her tighter.

As he gently kissed her cheeks and face and lips, she calmed. She felt her freshly washed hair caressing her neck and face. Zach's hands stroking her back, his words calming her brain. He had her. In the midst of all this turmoil, he had her.

"I'm not afraid," she told herself, willing herself to believe it.

"Baby, there's nothing there. There's no blood. Is anything burning?"

"My throat. But I'm scared," she whispered. "That's

why. I'm so sorry. Others need attention. We should help them."

Kim couldn't help herself. This was one of her worst fears. That she'd be horribly disfigured and alone. In her time as a judge, she'd seen several women who'd been set on fire by their mates, and heard their stories. Their pain had been heartbreaking. After hearing those cases, she'd had nightmares.

"It's okay to be scared. I'm right here. I won't let anything happen to you."

She rested her head against his chest and closed her eyes. The breeze, the closeness and the situation had all made her wish they were somewhere else, in another time and place, and they were free to be whomever they wanted to be. She could be Kim, the carefree day care owner who taught sign language to deaf children. Zach could be the hero crime fighter who pursued justice for innocent victims.

Tears seeped from beneath her eyelids, and, surprised, she shook her head in frustration. "I hate crying. What a stupid girl thing to do."

Sirens wailed in the background and Zach rested his head atop hers. "Girls cry all the time. Men wish they could cry like women do, then we wouldn't die so young."

Kim laughed silently. "That's the key to living longer? Crying?"

"Yeah."

Kim looked up at Zach. He was a man who didn't take any mess off anyone. He would never be afraid of her. She liked him for that.

"When I catch this person, I'm going to pull their limbs off, fry them and make them wish they'd gotten an honest job in sanitation."

"That's the sweetest thing a man's ever said to me." Kim ran her tongue along the inside of her cheek. "I appreciate you."

"I didn't do all this so someone could hurt you. They're going to pay."

The first squad car arrived along with an ambulance.

"I know. Thank you."

He eased her away from the others and backed her into the doorway of a nearby shop.

He shook his head no. "You're my only priority." In the secret place in her heart, where she'd stored love for all that she'd never have, Kim placed the unexpressed hope she felt for her and Zach. That they might one day experience true love.

Little girls were allowed to wish, and big girls were allowed to fantasize.

"We'll deal with 'us' later."

"Us" was something she thought he would never acknowledge. In the midst of all this turmoil, she was falling for her bodyguard.

The Hood van pulled up a second later. Zach lifted Kim inside, giving instructions to take her to the hospital. Ben got out just as two more APD patrol cars pulled up.

Rob was at the wheel of the van, and another van of Hood agents pulled up behind the officers. Rob stepped out and spoke to the officer in charge.

Zach had both of Kim's hands in his. "I've got to go, but I'll meet you at the hospital."

He turned away, but she grabbed his hand, trying to follow him out the door. "No, I'm not leaving. If I was hurt, I'd feel like that table looks."

They could all see inside the small restaurant that the place on the table where the ice cream had been was now a disintegrated hole.

"Zach, it would be insensitive of me to just leave. Why don't you go find Keon? I'll stay with Rob, okay? I promise to stick by his side. But I want to be here with you. I don't want to leave."

Rob interrupted and briefed Zach. When Zach turned back to Kim, her fear increased. "Rob, take her to Xan and have her checked out, then meet me back here."

"But—" Kim said.

"This is not up for debate. If you're sick and we wait, and something happens later, I'll never forgive myself. You're being a judge and not a client, and I need to think about your safety."

"Kim, I'll check on everyone else," Rob told her. "I'll let you know the bleeding woman's status later."

Zach helped Kim inside the van, secured her seat belt and closed the door.

Rob quickly pulled away, leaving Kim no choice but to go with the swiftly moving vehicle.

Chapter 8

"Zach closed the truck door before I could convince him. I'm not used to having my wishes denied." Although Kim knew he was acting in her best interest, she still felt frustrated and helpless. It had been three hours, and it was dark outside. She'd called his cell phone once, but Zach hadn't answered. Of course he was busy; her life was at stake.

Who was the person who'd tried to kill her? Was it Lieutenant Franklin? Why would he change his program from nighttime attacks to daytime? Why not at the house when there were less people around, and why try to hurt so many innocent people? Maybe he expected her to be with Clark.

It wasn't Franklin. He *knew* Clark was gone.

This had to be the other person or people. Zach had been right. There were two groups after her. They'd taken a helluva chance out in the open like that. Were they desperate? Why? What had she done to make someone want to kill her in such a heinous manner?

As the questions mounted, so did her discomfort. She needed to talk to Zach. She needed to be with him. Today their relationship had changed and she wanted to talk to him. She needed to figure things out with him. Never had she been so personally conflicted in all her life. Even though they'd been together when it happened, she'd felt safer with him than she did now with his sister.

Dr. Alexandria Hood, Zach's oldest sister, was a board certified general practitioner, and a member of the Hood Trap Team. Her focus was usually in catching husbands in compromising situations. However, she and her team of women had the same responsibility as Zach and the men of Hood Investigations; to protect all they served.

They were bodyguards, investigators, fathers and mothers. They were a family. Kim remained objective. That was the part where her parents had failed abysmally.

In the den, Xan handed Kim a glass of chardonnay and pointed a remote at a wall of blinking lights. A Keri Hilson song began to play softly in the background.

"Zachary is doing what's best for you."

Xan's assistant, Connie, who'd had been in Xan's home office during Kim's exam, brought some papers to Xan, then wished them both good-night. Xan reviewed the papers, then handed them to Kim.

"Your tests came back clean," the doctor explained.

"Add these results to your medical records and explain to your physician why these had been performed. As a matter of protocol, a copy of my progress notes was faxed to their office by Connie before she left."

Kim read every word of the tests, then folded the printouts and inserted them into her purse. "Thank you for getting these back so quickly."

"The tests didn't require us to wait long for the results. You only ingested trace amounts. Not enough to hurt your mouth, esophagus or stomach. Those amounts were flushed out by the milk I had you drink."

Kim rubbed her stomach. "I'm sure my bladder will thank you all night long. Come to think of it, I should probably eat something with this wine."

"Definitely. What do you feel like? I cooked dinner, but my kids are with their friends tonight."

The women strolled into the kitchen. "You cooked anyway?"

"Yeah. My brothers and Hugh will drop by. Hugh is still single, and he has to eat." Xan pulled out stuffed salmon with lemon, green beans and couscous.

Xan heated Kim a plate of food and served her on fine bone china. "I love this pattern," Kim complimented.

Xan ran her finger lovingly around the rim of her plate. "It was my mother's. I don't believe in saving my best for special occasions. Every day my boys walk in this house alive is special to me."

Kim's heart melted a little. *Her boys.* "Do you still think about them as being little?"

"Not often, but sometimes." Xan's tender smile

spoke volumes. "It's like they're mine ever since Victoria died."

The food was well flavored and hard to resist. "That's your mom?"

Xan nodded. "If I think *mom,* I'll cry. If I think *Victoria*—" she sat up with a very straight back "—then I can maintain my composure."

With no frame of reference from her own disjointed relationship with her mother, Kay, Kim felt compelled to question Xan more. "She couldn't have been too composed with all those boys. Twins, too. How'd she manage?"

"Victoria was a lady, a crusader, a compassionate, spiritual woman, who loved us tremendously. She was as we are. Different. The older boys were more thoughtful, but devilish. Mel and I were tough and feminine, and she helped us find a comfortable balance. Hugh was a bookworm, and she fostered his love of reading after his mom passed away.

"Zach was fearless. He was a funny boy who would roll around on the floor, and he would do anything to make her laugh. His heart was broken when she died. I didn't think he'd come back."

"Where'd he go?"

"He just disappeared. Zach," Xan said, tossing the oven mitts onto the counter, "was always a free spirit. He still won't tell us where he was. I know he was grown, but I thought of him as my oldest baby because he was my mother's youngest baby."

Kim had longed for that bond, but her parents had never wanted more children. They hadn't really wanted her. "How long was he gone?" she asked, the flavor leaving her food.

"Over a year."

"Oh, my goodness. You must have been worried sick."

"I was." Xan rubbed the back of her neck. "Then one day I came downstairs, and he was asleep on my stoop."

Kim was shocked. "Outside?"

Xan blinked rapidly, her eyes bright with tears. "Yes. Disheveled and thirty pounds lighter. I know he traveled, but what he did, I don't know."

"Wow." Kim's heart ached for him. "How long has it been? Is he all right?"

"Ten years, and no. Every year he goes away, but he comes back. That's all I ask of him. He has a room in every one of our houses. Just so we can keep an eye on him."

The idea of Zach being homeless was almost too much to bear. "Does he have a home?"

Xan tossed her microbraids over her shoulder. "Yes, but he hardly goes there. He only bought it as a tax deduction. We told him to buy a house or get married."

Kim choked on her wine. Xan offered her another napkin. "Sorry. That's a family joke." She looked regretful for having revealed so much of their personal lives.

Kim regained her composure and sipped the glass of water Xan had slid into her hand. "It doesn't bother me. Really, and I won't tell a soul what you've shared with me. I'm used to keeping secrets."

Xan looked grateful. "I really shouldn't go on about the past. He's here now and that's what counts. You probably get eaten up in taxes, too." Xan held up her hands and shook her head. "Sorry! I'm sorry. I'm not trying to sister you." They both laughed.

"'Sister me.' What's that mean?"

"Being the oldest in this family has its benefits and its drawbacks. I often feel compelled to butt in where my nose has no business."

"That's a big but, no pun intended. Okay, that didn't sound right." They shared a laugh again. "Marriage isn't for me, Xan. I work too much, so it wouldn't be fair to ask someone to join my world when I couldn't give them a fair amount of time."

"What about fair to you?"

"I'm okay," Kim reassured her.

"You're gorgeous, smart and you eat like a bird. If anything, you need someone to take care of you and you take care of him."

"I don't think he exists. That's why I'm single. I'm really okay."

Xan didn't look reassured, but she didn't say any more. "Come on, Ms. Okay. Let's get comfortable."

Kim walked around Xan's family room, jealous of the knickknacks that told stories, the pictures that reflected memories and the warmth that emanated from the room. The feeling couldn't be duplicated with the perfect purchase. There was a genuine spirit of wholesomeness in the room that came from family.

Kim and Xan had been at the house for three hours, and Kim wasn't at all bored with the very intelligent head of the Hood clan. But Kim could also see where Xan deferred to her brothers' wishes when it came to family and business. Kim perused a built-in shelf of photos. Gorgeous women stood next to the handsome Hood men. "Are these your brothers' wives?"

"Yes. The twins are newlyweds, and new fathers. It's been an exciting year for our family. What about you? Do you eventually plan to have children?"

Kim had given her medical history to the doctor before she'd been examined, so Xan knew she didn't presently have any children. "No, I won't have any. I've dedicated my life to practicing law."

"You're certainly young enough, or am I prying?" Xan asked. She stood, and Kim admired the woman, who was fit yet feminine. She seemed to have it all. The career, big house, husband and kids. She even had a dog.

"You're not prying. I almost made it to the altar once, but he chickened out. He thought we would have been living in a glass house, and he wanted a normal life. I couldn't argue with him there. I took issue with him waiting until I had the dress on at the church to tell me. I don't want to be a single mom, so no, I won't have children."

Xan curled up on the camel-colored suede sofa. "My brothers would have pulled that poor man apart for that escapade. It is hard to live a normal life as a public figure because people are constantly watching your every move. But if you have nothing to hide, you get used to the scrutiny. I'm a doctor, and I never drink in public. Ever. I don't need the women in my practice questioning my judgment because of something they've overheard from some talkative waiter."

Kim held up the glass of mineral water. "Neither do I. It's too risky. I don't do anything in public. I don't date," Kim confessed. "Too many of my friends have suffered for that momentary lapse in judgment when they let their honey of the day snap a picture of them in a compromising position. The political fallout has been tremendous."

"Wow. You'd think lawyers and judges would be smarter than that," Xan commented.

Kim shook her head. "We're just like everybody else. It's that momentary lapse in judgment that ruins careers. I didn't want that to happen to me. But I believe people should be able to have fun in their lives without it being front page news. So I decided to go it alone."

"What a sacrifice." Xan's eyes twinkled. "I'm getting you some more wine."

Kim giggled. "I'm fine with water."

"You can have fun tonight! My brother is driving, and you're not leaving until he gets here. You should be living it up until your situation changes."

Kim took the glass of chardonnay and enjoyed the smooth flavor. It had been too long.

Xan reclaimed her seat on the couch. "When I'm home, I forget all the cares of the world and completely relax. I have wine, I eat, I work out, I relax. We have parties with the entire family over. We have a blast. Do you ever miss not having someone next to you?"

Having had Zach around the past week had been different from her solitary existence. Different even from having Clark, her assistant, around. Zach didn't do things to please her. He did things that were right for her. They were distinctly different. She couldn't imagine what it would feel like to have someone around that loved her *and* did things for her. Her life would be passionate.

Kim started to answer, then heard the front door open and close. Voices bounced off the soft-pink-colored walls. They weren't quite arguing, but close.

"I hope we cashed her check before you nearly let her get killed."

"You exaggerate too much," Zach said casually. "She was covered at all times."

"Then how'd she almost get poisoned?" Hugh was defending Kim, and she was endeared to the quiet man. But Zach was right. He'd protected her every second. It was her fault for wanting to go there in the first place.

"Whoever it was had to have been there. Was there any video?" Zach shook his keys. Kim was accustomed to that sound. He was thinking as he talked.

"No. You were so careful," Hugh said sarcastically, "we got a nice shot of you smiling, Mr. Toothpaste, but none of your attempted assassin."

"I know what you need. A colonic to get that stress out of you," Zach told his cousin.

"Zach, you're being immature and irresponsible," Hugh said. "A dangerous combination."

"No, I'm not. I did everything I could to keep Kim out of harm's way. Nobody feels worse about that man getting to her than me. When are we getting the background checks on the office staff?"

"Got them today. You didn't check in until dinnertime, remember? You were in court all day."

"That's cool. We can go over them after Kim goes to sleep."

"Copy that," Hugh said.

Xan had watched her throughout the entire exchange, but Kim had perfected her poker face. She'd been a judge too long to allow her emotions to be revealed. However, she wanted to defend Zach. But the inroads they'd made... She had to see him.

Her heart raced as she heard Zach's footsteps getting closer. She was used to solving disputes, but she knew she was out of her element here. She couldn't intervene because she was the subject of the discussion.

She stood up, but Xan waved her down. "Enjoy your wine. This is going to be a long night, if that conversation is any indication. They must not know we're in the family room," she said loud enough for them to hear.

Kim sat but couldn't stay seated. Zach entered the room and she stood up again. Relief and gratefulness hit her in the chest, and all the words she wanted to say wouldn't come out. The attack had been directed at her, but because of her Zach was in harm's way, also. He was her bodyguard, but she felt a sense of responsibility for him, too. "Anything?" she managed.

"What is that?" He took her glass and smelled it. "Xan!" he chastised, drinking the wine himself and setting the glass on the coaster on the table.

When she stood up, he knew what she sought. His eyes told her not to worry, but she couldn't help it. His hands hovered near her waist, their new home, and she stepped closer.

Nothing new. You're safe. You're with me. All unspoken words, but she'd learned what the tilt of his lips meant, the slight uptick of his chin, the narrowing of his eyes and the slow blink. She knew when to move quickly and when she could possibly persuade him to her point of view. When had they started communicating in their own silent language? She couldn't stop looking at him. How his shoulders moved, his mouth. They hadn't found anything.

Xan watched them with open interest. "Kim's old enough for a glass of wine."

His hands found their home right above her hip bone. "Don't turn into a lush like my sister," he said teasingly.

"The same sister-doctor you insisted on sending me to. That's nice to know." Her hand found his.

"Your smart mouth wasn't burned by that acid, that's for sure." His gaze roamed her body in long sweeping strokes.

"You changed?" Zach asked.

"Yes," Kim said of her green above-the-knee skirt and gray-and-green sleeveless blouse. The skirt hugged her curves and the top played down the size of her boobs. She couldn't have asked for better clothing.

She looked up and there was hunger in Zach's eyes. Kim wished she had the audacity of some of the younger pop singers who flashed their hips at men, but she never forgot who and what she was. "It's not bad, is it?"

"There's nothing bad about it," Xan said, before Zach could articulate his feral thoughts.

He winked at his sister, returning from wherever his thoughts had taken him. "Is she really all right?"

Kim tipped his chin until he was looking at her again. "I'm much better."

"You're all right?" He stooped a little. "Open," he ordered, tilting her head back so he could personally inspect her mouth. Their bodies touched as if they were meant to.

Kim obeyed. "I'm good," she barely managed.

"Yeah?" Zach let her close her mouth. "God almighty." He pulled her head into his chest and exhaled into her hair before kissing the corner of her mouth and her nose. "I'm so glad. Xan, nothing's wrong with her stomach?"

"Relax, baby. She's in good shape. Blood tests were all negative. You both did a good job."

Kim's heart triple somersaulted in her chest. She didn't think Zach realized that he'd just kissed her in front of his sister and the very silent Hugh. Releasing her, Zach sat beside Xan and bear-hugged her before slobbering her cheek with kisses. She giggled and playfully swatted his butt.

"You're paying all the bills, buddy. Don't think kisses will get you out of this."

"I know. Thanks, big sis."

Kim had taken her seat again, and silently applauded herself for not falling down. Her equilibrium was off after being so affectionately accosted by Zach. His cousin sat on the double love seat, watching the lovefest, smiling.

"You good?" Hugh asked Kim.

Kim nodded. "Do you have any idea what happened? How did the person get in that store?"

"Well, it wasn't Keon. We found him in the back with a nice bump on the head. Poor kid got robbed of his tip, too. It seems the ice cream store hired a new person this week, Shelby Grant. She was the server who brought the sundae to your table."

"That didn't seem like a woman to me." Kim closed her eyes to focus on the person. As she replayed it in her mind, she realized she hadn't seen her face. "Her stature and tone of voice made me think it was a man. Had she been waiting all this time for me to come back?"

Zach shrugged. "We're still investigating. We've got her on several street cameras, but she avoids them cleverly. Like she knows them well. The chief is looking into whether she may work in the traffic department in some capacity or another."

"I'm shocked," Kim said.

"Don't be. He's going to want to be the first to go to the media if he catches this person. So he has to be involved. Anyway, you've been to that ice cream shop after work before. Often enough that she was right in assuming you'd stop by back there. My hunch is that she hasn't been following you, but she's been lying in wait for you to come in, and when you did, she took her chance."

"But you were there."

"She didn't recognize me. Besides, that's some kind of hate going on there. Think hard. Can you place her?"

Rubbing her arms, Kim shook her head. "No, but she smelled odd. Like she'd been cooking on a grill or something. She was tall and she walked with a hitch in her step."

"Maybe she'd just come from the shelter on Fourteenth Street. Sometimes they have cookouts." Hugh got up and headed toward the kitchen, coming back to top off their wine. "I'll call and see if they had one today before heading over there."

"Eat," Xan told her cousin. "There's salmon and vegetables in the warmer."

Zach was on the phone, while Kim drank her wine. It had made her relax too much. She felt content to allow Zach and Hugh to do all the work, and that wasn't like her at all.

Zach ended his call, then said, "Shelby Grant doesn't exist. As I said, she was waiting for you to come in to make her move. I'm heading back over to the restaurant. They found her uniform."

"What can that tell you?"

Kim had been leaning back on the couch, but now she sat forward.

"A lot. But I want you to stay here with Xan until I get back."

"No, Zach. I've imposed enough. I can ride with you." Kim tried to rise and bumped her chin on his shoulder by accident. "That's why I don't drink. I get clumsy."

"Have you eaten?" he asked, putting his arm around her.

"No. Yes. We ate a little while ago. I'm not hungry." Her stomach grumbled and she patted it. "Stop making me into a liar."

Though Kim knew that Xan was part of the Hood crime fighting team, Kim felt completely safe with Zach. She wished she could tell him how she felt without sounding ridiculous. She wished she could convey how worried she'd been that maybe she'd talked up her attacker, even though logic ran counter to that thinking. His gaze was nearly overwhelming.

"Do you always talk to yourself?"

"Yes, no." Kim sighed. "I'm about ready for bed. I have court tomorrow, and—"

"Court is starting late tomorrow because the building is being fumigated. So we don't have to rush. Just chill."

"Did you just tell a Superior Court judge to chill?" Her diction was perfect.

"Yep." How did he ignore her wishes and make it all right? *This is his territory,* Kim reminded herself. She couldn't do anything without him allowing her to.

"I don't have to do what you say." She sounded childish. First she praised him for rescuing her, then she had a tantrum. Why couldn't she make up her mind?

After all they'd been through, she was accustomed to Zach bringing her close to him. She was even used to him touching her. But she was surprised when his lips met hers and then moved with sensual intent over her lips. All of her defenses and objections crashed around her feet like crystals of ice. She was swept into a passion so engulfing, she couldn't believe a kiss could make her feel so desirous.

Zach pulled Kim to him and kissed her until her legs were weak. She didn't *want* to say anything else. She wished kissing him could go on, but this wasn't right. It just felt better than anything else she'd done for herself in the past. He broke the kiss and looked into her eyes.

"Xan," she said without looking at his sister. "Can we have a moment of privacy?" Kim heard her rather than saw her leave. When she was sure they were alone, her body surrendered to all the feelings of lust, and she tingled all over. Kim didn't move away from him, nor did she stroke his arms to bring herself closer as she wanted to. "What are you doing? You told me earlier today we couldn't be more than what we were, strictly professionals. What changed your mind, and when were you going to inform me?"

"When I saw you riding away in the van with Rob, I thought that could have been the last time I saw you, and that bothered me. I knew I would kiss you when I saw you again. We'll have to work out the rest. Not right now, though. I'll be back in an hour, then we can chill at home."

He squeezed her waist and released her. This time Kim had a hard time letting go.

Zach walked into the kitchen, and a few seconds later, he and Hugh walked out the door.

Xan brought in a platter of hors d'oeuvres and served Kim. "I guess you two came to an understanding."

Xan knew her brother was falling in love with Kim and Kim with him.

Kim didn't care. Her first kiss in two years wasn't going to be ruined by Zach's sister.

Kim licked her lips. She savored the tingling feeling and the memory of the pressure of his lips against hers.

The artichoke hearts on the tray looked inviting, but she passed on them. "I don't know what just happened to me, but I'm going to need more wine."

Xan laughed. "Oh, I know. You got Hood-hooked."

Kim didn't know what Hood-hooked was, but it sure felt good.

"Remind me to let it happen again."

Xan laughed. "You might not have a choice with Zach. When he makes up his mind, you're his."

Chapter 9

Zach checked on Kim while she slept, and wished like hell he could solve her case and then climb into bed with her. She was the type of woman he considered to be a life changer.

That's what was happening to him. He was changing, and he didn't know what to do about it. As he stood in the doorway of her room at 3:00 a.m., he knew that Kim was the only woman who had ever made him laugh and think hard at the same time. He was filled with admiration for her, and he'd never felt that before for a woman outside of his family.

Kim was tough. Tougher than any woman the Hood team had ever worked with.

She wasn't an emotional woman in the typical sense. She didn't cry at things that made most women cry. All day she heard gruesome details about the failings of mankind, and she didn't shed a tear. All day she listened to how we recklessly disposed of each other's love and lives once they were no longer useful. She viewed pictures of horrible atrocities at the hands of man, and she looked into the face of evil and unspeakable grief with equal fairness and compassion.

Kim had no one. No family to fall back on, no one at home to help relieve her stress. Yet she still walked out of the courtroom each day, holding his hand, her phone and purse in the other, asking if she could go outside and soak up a little bit of sun. That was all. Her life was so simple, and she didn't expect any more from it.

Zach didn't understand her simplicity. He understood depression, sadness and bitterness. Anger, frustration and pity were emotions he knew well. But acceptance?

He had a hard time with that one. How could someone accept the fact that they were the last of their family on earth? She'd accepted her life of no family, and she moved on.

That was absolutely unthinkable to him. He needed every member of the Hood clan. Without them he'd be nothing.

Zach closed her door and settled down to review their day.

Court had been difficult today, with both sides pushing the legal envelope.

Whenever there had been a fight between opposing counsel, Kim had waded into the middle, and she didn't back down, either. Nobody got away with anything in her courtroom, and Zach could see why she was hated among defense attorneys.

Today the prosecutor had tried her patience. He'd questioned several witnesses until the court practically knew their life stories. The judge had forced him to move on. "If this persists, I'll have your cocounsel examine your witnesses. Pick up the pace," she'd told him.

He'd heeded the warning, and when he'd run out of witnesses, he had come clean. "My star witness hasn't arrived. Can we have a short continuance so we can ascertain his whereabouts?"

"No. The court has been very indulgent. You've wasted enough of our time. Call your next witness."

"But this is a key witness to the prosecution's case, Your Honor. We ask for the court's indulgence in giving this witness another fifteen minutes."

"Your request is denied. Move on," she'd warned.

Losing his composure, the prosecutor had slammed his hand on the table and glared at the judge. "Judge, Mr. Bryson is a drug dealer. He's going to spend the rest of his life in prison. What's another fifteen minutes?"

"Objection," the defense attorney had interrupted. "Is the prosecution on his own witness list to testify?"

The judge had nodded. "Sustained. Watch yourself. Present your next witness."

He'd twirled a pencil, his mouth twisted in a cocky grin. "They haven't arrived yet. I planned on questioning my witness until the end of the day. I plead with the court for a continuance to try to contact him."

"Again, denied. This isn't your first time trying a case. You either present your next witness or rest your case." Kim had pulled off her glasses, and Zach knew that meant she had lost her patience.

Angry with the judge's decision, the prosecutor had turned toward the gallery. "The prosecution calls Mrs. Constance Bryson."

"Objection." The defense attorney had stood. "I'm confused as to why the prosecution would call the defendant's mother. She has no knowledge of anything pertinent to this case. She's seventy-five, and she was out of town when the incident in question occurred."

"I won't know what she knows until I question her." The prosecutor had raised a sheet of paper. "She's on the prosecution's witness list."

The judge had motioned to both attorneys. "Approach. If this is a stall tactic, you'll be held in contempt of court and thrown into jail," she'd warned the prosecutor. "The motion is overruled. Step back."

Within five questions, Zach had known it was indeed a stall tactic, and the judge hadn't been gentle. The prosecutor was still in jail, as Kim slept through the night.

Zach closed the door to Kim's room and went back to his post in the living room of her house. The background checks on her staff had come back clean, except one. Trevor Mason, her assistant. He'd been filling in for Clark this past week, but lately Kim had been doing all the administrative work herself. Trevor had been calling in sick, and Zach needed to know why.

He sent texts to his brothers and Hugh, asking them to check into Trevor Mason's whereabouts, and then he closed his eyes. He needed at least four hours of sleep so he'd be fresh for the next day.

"Mr. Stuckey, are you ready to proceed?" Returning to the courtroom the next day, Zach observed the prosecutor, who showed no signs of having been locked up the night before. He was calm and well composed.

"Call your first witness," Judge Thurman told Prosecutor Stuckey, who stood at his table, his signature Montblanc pen in hand.

"I'd like to call Marshal Howard Daniels to the stand."

"Sidebar," the defense attorney said, staying seated, following procedure.

"Approach," Kim said. Zach watched from the left side wall as the attorneys approached the bench. Two deputies stood near the defendant, while the other six, who were stationed around the room, held their positions.

"The witness isn't on the list," Zach heard the defense attorney tell the judge.

"Yes, he is. Unnamed witness one. I faxed this to you last night. You received it at 8:01 p.m. For his safety, I couldn't use his name."

"The witness will be allowed to testify. Step back," the judge ordered.

Questioning began easy enough, the marshal an older man of fifty-four. He knew what information to give and how to give it. "The defendant called my home and offered me a deal. He wanted a cell phone brought to him inside the jail. He would pay me three hundred dollars."

"Did you take him the phone?"

"No. I turned the information over to my superior officer, who told me to tape any subsequent conversation. When the defendant called back, I taped the call."

"Objection. The tape could have been tampered with."

"Sustained."

"How did you go about securing the call?"

The officer looked at the judge, then back at Stuckey. "I have a family member who works at Quantico, Virginia, where they have the best equipment for this sort of thing. I had that family member come and set up the equipment for the call and record it. It was then analyzed through their department in Quantico so no one could say I tampered with the calls. It has been sealed and is ready to be delivered now."

"How do you know it's ready to be delivered, Mr. Daniels?"

"As I told your office, you would have to call and make them aware of my date to testify, and they would make the tapes available to you."

Stuckey turned to the judge. "Your Honor, I'd like to sign into evidence the audio tapes of the defendant and Marshal Howard Daniels."

"I'll allow."

The doors of the court opened and two FBI agents entered and presented the evidence, which was signed for by Stuckey. The defendant slipped lower in his chair.

"With your permission, Your Honor, I'd like to play these tapes."

"Would the prosecution like a short continuance to review them?"

"No, ma'am."

The tapes played the damning evidence of the defendant asking the marshal to bring him money, a phone and drugs. He made mild threats. The defendant became agitated with his attorney when he didn't object to certain parts of the tape. The judge ordered him to be quiet and the tape continued. Everyone in the court heard him offer the marshal ten thousand dollars to kill Judge Thurman. He spoke of having someone on the inside of her house, who would make her death look like an accident. He spoke of the glass in her windows being worth a fortune. The judge ordered the tape stopped.

The defense argued the tapes' admissibility, and when he was overruled, he asked for a mistrial and for the judge to recuse herself. She told them she would recess court until the next day.

Kim went to her new chambers and lay down in the dark. They were close. Now she knew the defendant wanted her dead. But Lieutenant Franklin had been instrumental in nearly killing her. But he didn't know they knew. Marshal Daniels was the good guy.

She had other cases to focus on, but she didn't have the energy. Her life could be over and she was only thirty-four.

The door opened and closed. "Judge?"

"Zachary?"

"What are you doing?"

"Lying down, trying not to have a pity party."

"Come on." He crossed to her and sat beside her. She turned on her side and her eyes filled with tears.

"I may be alone in this world, but I don't want to die."

"You're not alone."

"You're right. I have Clark. He'll be back in five days."

"You've got me. And my brother's dog. Just give the word." Zach stroked her hair. "It's not easy hearing someone so casually wants to end your life, but he's a criminal. He's got only one thing going for him and that's being a bad person. The only thing this guy regrets is getting caught."

"I matter, Zach," she whispered. "I help people." Her voice caught.

Zach lifted her and pulled her into his arms. "You matter to me."

Her arms slid around his neck and he held her tight against him. "No, Zach. You keep bringing me to this point, then pushing me away. I feel like I'm that wide-eyed soon-to-be bride again, waiting for my fiancé to show, and he doesn't. You have to want me all the way, or not."

"Marriage?" he asked, his face buried in her bosom.

Kim pulled on his ears and he looked her in the eye. "No. I'm not going there again." As she finished the words, her stomach rumbled. "Commit to—" she considered her words "—liking me."

"I do like you. A lot. This case is complicated and it's going to become even more so before it's over. Liking you and really *liking you* could get us both into real trouble. Do you understand?"

"Yes." She kissed him, her tongue probing his lips, meeting his tongue in a wonderful dance of pleasure and passion. He groaned and she giggled. He squeezed her bottom and she pressed into him. This was the man she wanted to get to know. The man with biceps bigger than her hands. Lips that brought tingles of pleasure to her cheeks and mouth, and thoughts of erotic pleasure to her mind.

She held on to Zach and buried her face in his neck. She wasn't going anywhere.

Chapter 10

"Zach, we've got something on Lieutenant Franklin from the judge's security detail. We need to meet with you and Kim this morning."

Zach stopped shaving and looked at his mini notebook. His cousin was on the screen, giving him the morning updates. Technology was sometimes intrusive, but today it was necessary. Had it not been for Hugh, he'd still be asleep and that would be bad. His dreams had been deep and seductive.

"This sounds serious," Zach said, his voice scratchy with sleep.

"It is pretty serious. If I'm right, this could affect—" He held up his hands. "Let's meet over breakfast. I'll sweep her house for listening devices and check on the progress of the renovations. We can talk over coffee. I've got a great blend I think the judge will like."

Zach smiled. "She's going to love you. See you in an hour."

Kim sipped her coffee, and Zach could see she was in her own world, the cup nestled in her palms, her eyes hooded. She was hooked. He wanted to take the deep blue mug from her and see if she'd throw a tantrum. She'd probably have him arrested. She gave him a side-long look. "What?"

"You're enjoying that coffee too much."

"I love coffee. Everybody has their vices. You love—" she hesitated over a long sip "—bossing me around. Where's Hugh and the rest of the team?"

"On the way in now. He stepped out to make sure the security door responded to the remote. Why aren't you dressed?"

Kim loosened the string on the silk robe and showed him her fuchsia A-line dress with the thin black belt. "I don't want to get food on it."

She looked good, like in his dream. Beautiful. Her hair was done and her makeup perfect. All night long their kiss had played on his mind, and he'd wished for a repeat so badly he'd slept poorly.

He snuck in a few kisses, but before they could get into anything hot and heavy, the door opened and his brothers walked in with Ice, their security agent recruiter.

Ever since Rob and Ben had started their families, the company had needed more agents, and Ice was the perfect individual for that job. Zach had to table his desire.

Rob shook Kim's hand. "Judge Thurman, this is Ice."

"Nice to meet you," the tall woman said, with a warm smile and a firm handshake.

"Please excuse how I'm dressed," Kim said about her robe. "I don't want to mess up my work clothes."

"No problem," Ice told her, partial to jeans and a hoodie. Ice was a master at blending in. She'd recently cut off her dreads and now sported a short fade haircut that made her look like one of the guys. "You should be comfortable in your own home."

Suddenly, it mattered to Kim that the kitchen was warm and cozy and that there were enough spaces at the exquisitely decorated table. Zach was the only guest who had ever sat there.

"Can I get anyone anything? Coffee, tea?" Kim offered. She rushed over and pulled some of the plates off the table. Zach took them from her hands and put them back, while Hugh dished up bagels, fruit and smoked salmon.

"This was last minute, so we brought everything," Ben said as he poured coffee. Hugh set up the computer for everyone to see, while Rob synced his phone to the computer.

Kim watched the Hoods work together in her kitchen, in her home, and she felt good. This was what it was like to have a family.

Even when her parents had been alive, she hadn't eaten with them.

She ate alone and they ate together.

Zach put the sugar bowl and cream on the table. A lump swelled in her throat. She liked having them in her house.

"You okay?" Ice asked her quietly.

"Yes, I'm good. What do you do for the Hood team? No offense, but you don't look like a Hood."

Ice laughed. "I'm not a Hood by blood, but I do enjoy working with these thugs." The men stopped, each holding a piece of her fine china, and Kim had to suppress a giggle. "At least they're good-looking," Ice added.

"I say pay cut," Rob told Ben.

"I'd just take all the bullets for their guns." Ice stood her ground, and Kim liked her even more.

"Definitely." Ben cast a conspiratorial wink at Ice and focused on the computer screen that Hugh was working on. "We'll get started as soon as Hugh gets everything pulled up."

Kim glanced at Rob and Ben and Hugh. They were great men, too.

But Zach… He'd kissed her when she'd been at his sister's house, but hadn't said a word about it since. She'd intentionally put it out of her mind because he'd been business as usual, but with all of them there, it was hard not to think about being a Hood.

There was no denying it; he was gorgeous. But he was a man. He made decisions and, honestly, his decisions took pressure off her that she hadn't known was part of her life. She slept easier knowing he was in the house, and when she left the bench each day, taking his hand had become something she looked forward to.

Now his family had invaded her home, and she was

enjoying herself. Not for the reason they were there, but *just because* they were there.

"Ice, would you like some coffee?"

"No, thanks. I'll get wired and stay that way all day. I'm here because I'm in charge of the assembly of our security team. I need to know how many agents are needed, and then I'm off to the next job. Hugh?"

"We're all set," he finally said. "The judge, whose code name is Themis—she was the Greek goddess of law—has to be on the bench in ninety minutes, so let's get started."

Ben patted a chair for Kim and she sat down as Hugh angled the computer screen for everyone to see. "Judge Thurman, you have a security breach. We know the defendant was in touch with Daniels. He went undercover and got the information to close the defendant down. The problem is that Franklin is on the run."

"What?" Disbelief rocked her. "He's going to lose his job. He'll be prosecuted and go to jail. What he's done is a career ender. Why?"

Kim knew about corruption, but for an agent of hers to do something so overtly against the rules, there had to be a good reason. Hugh pulled up photos of Franklin. He looked like a nice guy, but that meant nothing.

"Could be blackmail, hardship or just greed."

"That's ridiculous. He has a family," Kim argued as if that would change their actions.

"Inmates with money and power buy off guards because they can be bought. Guards make decent money, but it's not great," Hugh told her. "So, for a little extra cash, some might sneak in cell phones, drugs and other contraband."

Kim rose, thinking. "That doesn't make good sense. The same guards in court aren't the same guards that take them into custody at the jail. What did he have to gain?"

Ben had been tapping his pencil eraser on the table ledge. "If he'd been successful in killing you, he would have gotten a new trial. Maybe witnesses would have been unavailable. I'm sure you've seen all of this before."

Kim bit her lip. "I'm not fully convinced. Why didn't the chief investigate these officers?"

"He supposedly did, according to the U.S. Attorney. Now they're investigating him. We're letting them handle that piece, and we performed a thorough investigation. Lieutenant Franklin has had the most contact with the defendant, Edward Bryson. Daniels has clean hands. He was smart, too."

"Okay. Now, is the lieutenant contacting the defendant, or vice versa?"

Hugh shook his head. "No, the opposite. The defendant's called Franklin several times in the middle of the night when his family was asleep. He was somehow given a phone in jail, and he called the lieutenant."

"We understand the Daniels piece, but why did Bryson turn to Franklin? What's he asking for?"

The Hoods looked from one to another.

Rob spoke up first. "Wiretapping is illegal, but we do it because we don't intend to prosecute anyone. We use the evidence to stay one step ahead of the bad guys and to keep our clients safe."

"But if the evidence is needed later, it's tainted and we can't take it to the police," Hugh added.

Kim reached to put her cup on the counter and Zach took it from her hand, helping her up. "Thank you, Zach. Don't tell me any more. Let me think about this." Kim walked around the kitchen. "How did you learn there were calls between the lieutenant and the defendant?" She held up her finger. "Be careful how much you tell me."

"In the process of doing background checks on all the employees, we ran checks on cell phones, house phones, social networking sites, visitors, emails and faxes. This is standard operating procedure and within the guidelines of our authority," Rob explained.

Hugh waved his pen and took over. "Everyone checked out. However, in two instances, we couldn't find the originating owners of several calls." Diagrams flipped into view on the computer. "I then traced the cell tower usage between the calls, and they were all from the jail to the home of the lieutenant."

"Stop! I can't know any more." Kim pointed to Rob. "Now we need a warrant. We can't legally put the phone in the defendant's hand. The warrants will give us permission to listen to their conversations. Use your own judge. You do have one, don't you?"

Rob smiled. "I do. Judge Julian Crawford."

"If you're talking about Julian Sr., you'd better hurry because he's about to retire. In fact, his family is throwing a huge retirement party for him. Julian's son offered to escort me." Kim walked to the built-in desk in the kitchen and pulled out an embossed invitation that flaunted the Crawfords' crest.

"Nice," Ice admired, touching the gold-and-green insignia on the back of the envelope.

"In high school, we used to kick all those Crawford boys' asses in football," Zach told Ice, flicking the envelope. "They finally learned to write in cursive. 'Bout time."

Jealousy had always been an emotion Kim had been objective about because it had never been directed toward her, but to see Zach jealous was empowering.

Kim slid the envelope under her nose, watching Zach. She sniffed it and handed it to Ben.

"You need to be careful. It's probably got some old-man liniment on it," Zach said sarcastically.

Kim and Ice giggled. "Zach, she's playing with your goofy head," Ice told him.

"I'm not going to see Pops Crawford. I'm going to see Baby Julian," Rob interjected. "Julian Jr. can't play football anymore. That's not his sport. It's basketball. Their sons played football."

Rob referred to his friend of more than twenty years as "baby," but anybody who knew Julian knew better. In his football playing days, he was an unstoppable tight end who could outrun anybody on the field.

Though Julian was older than Rob by only two years, he'd mentored the young attorney through law school. He was also six-four and had daughters as tall as he.

Ben rubbed his new knee. "I can't play football, either. I'll roll with you. Zach is the only fool in the family still trying to catch passes. Listen, I reviewed Kim's schedule for today, and she's scheduled to rock the babies from seven to eight. Given yesterday's events, I'd take four agents to the hospital."

Rob nodded his head in agreement. "Ice, if you have any questions, call me. I'll be at the Crawford estate."

"Got it. Have a great day. Judge," Ice said, extending her hand. "Nice to meet you."

"You, too." Kim shook her hand and watched the family disassemble what had taken them ten minutes to create. The family unit for them was natural. It was part of the Hood DNA.

Ben and Rob walked outside, leaving Hugh, Zach and Kim. Hugh quietly packed up his equipment while eating.

"I don't think it's a good idea to go to the hospital to rock the babies today," Zach told Kim as she refilled her coffee cup. "Not after the ice cream store incident. We can't put more lives in jeopardy. I'm sorry."

"Are you saying no?" Kim asked him.

He shook his head. "I'm using my best judgment and saying I don't think it's a good idea."

Zach turned around to see Kim cooking her salmon on the stove.

"It's cooked already. It's smoked."

"I don't like the texture when it's like that. I really want some bacon, but Flora keeps buying stuff that isn't even meat."

"Will you marry me?" Hugh asked Kim.

Kim smiled at him. "No. We'd both die of heart disease, and I couldn't bear to lose my husband that way."

He stopped moving. "You're smooth. Really, that was a good answer." He tapped his computer. "Judge, I got a print back from the window in the keeping room, but it doesn't match anything. I'm going to keep running it. I noticed that your subdivision has cameras at the entrance."

"They're fake. We did it to keep the bad people out."

Hugh chuckled. "You rich people are hilarious. If someone really got hurt, the outcry would be tremendous. Fake cameras? You ought to be ashamed of yourselves."

"We are," she said, looking suitably ashamed. "I'm in trouble and they could've helped me. We're arrogant. That's all there is to it, and it's costing me now. Not just what I paid you, but my assistant was hurt and I could get killed. But that's why you're here. Once we get the warrants and the information, we need to take the information to the police chief, if he still has a job."

Rob agreed as he and Ben came back inside. "I think he's ignorant, but he has clean hands. He needs to be brought back into the loop. Zach, you're riding ghost."

"Negative. I can't just sit by and let you all do all the heavy lifting. I'll go crazy."

"Zach," Rob said, his voice firm, "you left the Thai restaurant with no backup. Serious security breach."

"True, but every other move has been by the book. Every one of you has had that one case when you used bad judgment. The judge is headstrong, but I'm in charge, Rob. We do things according to procedure. All the security checks have been completed according to policy. If you don't look at that one time, I've done everything according to plan. Ghost is when the real challenges occur, and if I need to be ghost, I will. The judge and I work well together. Give me my assignment and I'll do what needs to be done."

Rob considered his brother's words, and Kim waited anxiously. A problem solver by nature, she wanted to jump in and defend Zach, but she knew she'd be out of line. Whatever the responsibility of being ghost was, Zach didn't want any part of it.

"Let me talk to Ben for a minute."

Ben and Rob stepped out of the kitchen. A few seconds later, Zach joined them.

Kim watched the dynamics, but kept quiet. The Hoods were cohesive. They flowed like a river. Even and calm at times, turbulent and choppy at others, but even when they disagreed, it was respectful, not like the courtroom, where everyone was trying to win at all costs.

The three reentered the kitchen, having come to an understanding.

"What's the decision?" Hugh asked.

Rob nodded, gathering his papers. "Zach is still active. I've got to get back. DaKota can't stand to be without her daddy."

"You just want to get home to look at her because she's so pretty," Ben told him, his hands shoved in his pockets, a grin on his face.

Although Rob's chest was poked out, they still ribbed on him. "I admit it. I made a gorgeous baby."

"She looks like her mother," Ben told Kim. "He had nothing to do with it."

"You're going to hurt his feelings." Glad to be included, she noticed that Zach held back and stayed across the room.

Rob was at the door. "They can't hurt me. Ben's ugly and he knows it. I'm sorry for my brothers and cousin, but their future kids don't stand a chance because DaKota is brilliant as well as beautiful."

Ben laughed hard. "Would you believe I'm riding with this bighead?"

"I don't think there's enough room in the car for you," Kim told him between giggles.

"I keep his head out the window. A truck will come by and—" he made a snapping sound "—pop this big balloon."

"That's mean," Kim chided.

"I had a baby the same day as him. Do you hear me telling the world my baby can speak Mandarin? No, because I have class."

Zach opened the kitchen cabinet, and as Ben turned, he bumped his head on the door.

"Okay, class, let's go," Rob told his brother, laughing. "See you tonight, Kim. Be safe."

"I will, Rob. Don't worry."

Having had enough of their shenanigans, Hugh snapped his fingers. "Can we focus? Zach, I'll start the background checks on the hospital staff today. That's a lot of people. Rob, I may need additional help once the checks start coming in. I'll start in Neonatal, the department the judge works in. Judge, you have forty minutes to report to work."

"Thank you, Hugh."

Rob had Ice on the phone. "Put three agents on the entries and exits to the hospital. Clear it through their security first."

"I'll help you," Zach offered, shrugging at Rob, who had put away his phone and had asked silently what was wrong with Hugh. "Let me know when. Come back here later tonight."

"No, we'll be imposing," Rob said. "Come to my house tonight. You can see DaKota."

"All right, cool," Zach said, straightening up the table, but Kim stopped him.

"It's no imposition," Kim told them. "I've never had this many people in my house before. It's kind of nice. So, in the future, please come back."

"We just got a dog who chews up everything." Ben looked hopeful. "I can drop her off and forget where I left her."

Kim's smile was quick. "Zach won't let me have a dog, sorry."

"Was that a lie, Judge?" he challenged her.

She put up her fingers to indicate just a teeny one. "Thank you, gentlemen. See you tonight."

She forked more salmon onto her bagel and added a dab of cream cheese before biting.

"Want some?" She held it out to Zach and let him have a bite.

"You're always feeding me," he said. When he was finished biting, she licked her thumb.

"I just have to brush my teeth. I'll hurry. What's the deal about riding ghost?"

"Nothing. You just don't do much and that can get a man into trouble."

"What kind of trouble?"

His gaze darkened and she knew his trouble was something that would intrigue her.

"The kind that causes mistakes. It's better for both of us if I stay active and out in the field, rather than holed up with you."

"Would we really be a mistake?"

"Yes, because when I'm focused on a private relationship, I'm there one hundred percent. The same goes for a case. Right now, you're a case. I don't mean to make it sound so cold, but…"

"Finish your sentence. We're both grown-ups."

Every bit of her wanted to know what he was going to say. She was so attracted to him. Not because of what he was, but who he was. He was his own man. He wasn't intimidated by her position, but attracted to her as a woman. That made her feel sexy and desirable. And the fact that he was fighting his attraction to her made her want him even more.

He stood across from her, the space in the kitchen seeming to widen. "Having the perfect affair doesn't seem like such a bad idea. But it would ruin your career and possibly get you killed because I wouldn't be able to focus all my energy on both."

"So let me get this straight. You can ride ghost and be in the background of the investigation, focusing all your attention on me, while the others do more of the legwork."

"Right."

"Or you can maintain our professional relationship, knowing we're attracted to one another."

"My first obligation is to keep you safe."

"Zach, have you ever felt this way about anyone else?"

He leaned back against the counter and drummed his fingers on the surface. "No."

"Then I'll respect your wishes." Kim loosened the sash on her robe, but then decided to wash the few dishes in the sink, a plan working in her brain. She was safe in her home. More than safe. Zach and his merry band of Hood relatives had made her home into a fortress, and thanks to her stalker, now the APD had her house under constant surveillance. Nobody in their sick mind was getting in here. At least here at home, she and Zach could enjoy each other safely. Out in the street, she'd play by his rules, but at home, he'd play by hers.

"Kim, I don't want you going to the hospital tonight."

"Zach, your job is to protect me, not keep me trapped in a castle. It's simple, really, and as you've pointed out, your job. Tonight's my night. I'm going. I'll be ready to go in five minutes."

Chapter 11

Court had been tedious and difficult.

More than once Zach had wanted to shoot both the defense and the prosecuting attorneys for being petty and wasting time. Judge Thurman had chastised the prosecution for prodding emotional jurors who'd refused to look at gruesome pictures of what the defendant's drugs had done to several victims. His relentlessness had cost him favor with the court, but he'd pressed forward.

Both a man and woman juror had broken down, begging the judge to be released from jury duty. She'd cleared the courtroom, speaking to the twelve jurors and two alternates, trying to gauge their mental stability. If she released them, going forward, she'd risk not having enough jurors should anything else happen, and the end result would be a mistrial. She'd reminded them of their civic duty and that they'd already given their word to fulfill their obligation for the trial.

The evidence of how the defendant had allegedly murdered the young woman for stealing the cocaine had been too much for the male juror. He'd wanted off and after stating his position, the judge had no choice but to excuse him.

The woman juror had decided to stay, but had asked that the defense attorney not stare at her and to no longer hand her the gruesome photos of the mutilated victim. The attorney seemed slimy, in her opinion. Though Kim personally agreed, she'd reminded juror eight to decide the case based upon the facts only.

Kim left the bench at six-fifteen, moving a lot slower than usual. She was tired, and when she reached for Zach's hand, it was as much to lean on as to hold.

"You're exhausted." He touched the small of her back, then applied pressure to the tight areas.

"Yes." Inside the door of her office, she stepped out of her shoes. Heading for the couch, Kim sat down and put her feet up, her head back, as she sighed long and loud.

"What is it, Kim?" He'd never seen her this way. Emotional, spent and in need of something he couldn't give her. He thought she was going to cry. Tears he could handle, but the moaning…he didn't know what to do about that. He moved toward the sofa. "Tell me how to help you. What is it?" he asked.

"I can't say it." Another long, loud moan escaped. Unsure what to do, Zach watched her make the wounded animal sound again. "What can I do?" he asked, sitting down and stroking her hair.

"Take my hair down for me," she whispered, her eyes glassy.

"Was it the attorneys?" He stroked her hair, massaging her scalp. "I can have them eliminated," he offered.

"No." Another moan started in her belly. "But what a sweet offer."

"What is it, then?"

She finally looked at him and wiped her eyes. Her fingers were wet, but there were no more tears. "We're supposed to be stronger, impartial and nonjudgmental, but sometimes…"

Zach hadn't seen any of the evidence, but he knew the last thing she'd seen were the pictures of the woman's mutilated body. How could she not be affected?

Zach did what he knew best and pulled her into his arms. "You going to cry?"

"Not likely," she said, her voice thin and soft. "I just hate this feeling."

"Tell me about it."

"Helpless. Tired. Weary." He held her for a while, comforting her until the moans slowed.

"I know what you need," he told her.

"Don't tell me sex," she said, giving him a lopsided grin.

"Do you think I'm some kind of animal?" He held her so tightly he feared he'd break her, but Kim squeezed him back.

"No. I was kidding. Bad joke." She moved, with some reluctance, out of his grasp and stood up.

"Hold out your arms. Legs apart, bend your knees and breathe."

"I need yoga?" she asked. "Cho's pose?"

"Yes, yoga. You're wound too tight and stressed out. Yoga will do you good. Ten minutes and we're going to the hospital."

Kim did as she was told, and ten minutes later she had to agree—she felt better. She also attributed her recovery to watching Zach work out in front of her. There was something sexy about a man standing in the prayer position.

"I feel better," she told Zach, her spirit and her body more at peace.

Zach sat on the couch. "You've got thirty minutes. I'll check my messages while you do your thing over there."

"Fine with me." Calmer, Kim sat at her desk and tried to get work done, but the amount of paperwork overwhelmed her. "I can't wait for Clark to get back. Where's Trevor? This trial schedule makes no sense." She pushed a button on the phone on her desk. "Trevor?"

Zach watched her from the comfortable sofa across the room. "Don't get all riled up again. He quit."

"What?" Kim put the handful of papers down. "When did that happen?"

"Three days ago."

"Why didn't anyone tell me?" Shocked, Kim looked around her office and saw the disarray. She got up and put the shoes she'd worn that day in the closet, bringing out another pair. Suit jackets from the previous days were still strewn across the office chairs, likewise for other discarded shoes. She walked around quickly, cleaning up after herself.

"Why didn't you tell me, Zachary?"

"Stop. You just finished relaxing. You've been busy with your case, and I've been busy watching you. I don't care about your office."

"I'm not talking about that. I need Trevor to make sure these are date-stamped that my office received them. If they're not, cases could be dismissed. Never mind. He couldn't have called me? I'm that horrible a boss that he couldn't have just said something to me? Like I don't deserve some consideration."

Kim glanced at her watch, hurried over and stabbed her feet into her heels. "I can do this myself. I just need to find the stamp."

"His office is by your old office. I'll go."

"No." Kim waved her hand, cutting him off. "You won't know what you're looking for."

Zach stood to his full height. "I'm pretty sure a college dropout like me can find a stamp. Stay here and don't unlock the door for anyone."

Zach walked out and Kim could feel the humiliation of her words ringing in her ears. She wanted to say she hadn't meant it that way, but in a way she had. He didn't know what the stamp looked like, and she knew she could find it faster than him. Her words hadn't meant to be a put-down, but a statement of fact.

With more speed than she thought possible in a man his size, he was back with a box of stamps, the stamp she needed in front. "I wasn't implying anything. I've never said anything like that."

"You chose the wrong words."

"I'm sorry. Okay?" She touched his arm. "What's wrong with you?"

The back of his jaw tightened and he grabbed her pashmina. "Nothing. You ready to go?"

"Yes," she said, putting the stamp in her bag along with the stack of papers. They left the office, silence between them. "What is it, Zach?"

"Nothing."

"Aren't you suspicious about Trevor leaving so abruptly? I'm calling him."

"Some people are inconsiderate, Kim. And honestly, Clark called this out long ago, but you glossed it over. He'd been taking long breaks, and taking days off. He wasn't loyal to you. He quit. Let him go. Besides, having him followed has turned up nothing."

Once in the SUV, Kim leaned back in her seat and let his words sink in. Still, she was annoyed. Who did he think he was, just quitting with no notice? He could forget a recommendation. The selfish brat.

Driving through the streets of Dunwoody, Kim appreciated the serenity of the trees and browning grass. The Bermuda grass was growing dormant for the winter, and landscapers were now aerating the hardening ground, while other home-care workers were beginning to string lights for upcoming Halloween celebrations, which were in two weeks. She'd never celebrated Halloween. Having gone to school in Switzerland, she'd celebrated All Saints' Day—as the Swiss did—a practice she had maintained even as an adult.

Kim honored her parents on All Saints' Day by cleaning their graves.

The top of the hospital came into view. They were about five minutes away. "Zach, I appreciate everything you've done for me. I'm just feeling hectic and frazzled. I didn't mean to be insensitive, but you have thicker skin than that. What's going on?" They pulled into the parking lot and Kim waited for the Hood agents to meet her at the car. She held up her hand before the agent could open the door. Zach signaled to them and they stood by the car, but turned their backs to the vehicle.

"I want you to listen to me. I'm not feeling sensitive. You're becoming insensitive and you're pushing back."

"I'm busy and this is getting to me. You can't expect me to sit still and let this take over my life."

"You hired me to do a job. Nobody said it would be easy. We need a little more time, but we're making progress."

"I'm frustrated."

"I know, but watch me while we're in there. That's all I'm asking. Eventually this person is going to strike again, and when they do, I want you to be ready. I don't want to lose you."

Kim unclenched her hands. He was right. She'd been pushing to live a normal life and probably making his job difficult, but was that wrong? She'd debate the temerity of her decision later. "You keep telling me and it's like I'm hardheaded. I'm sorry, Zach."

He looked at her and before she almost lost her nerve, she leaned over and kissed him on the cheek. "I hear you. You won't lose me." His agents were still turned away from the car.

"We'll finish this later," he said. "Let's move out."

He knocked on the window, the door was opened and Kim was rushed inside the hospital.

Seeing Kim in pink hospital scrubs holding the baby moved Zach emotionally. He'd been with her for nearly three weeks and had feelings for her he realized were so personal and sexual, he should just walk away now. Clients had tested him, they had even exasperated him before, but he hadn't taken it personally. He'd certainly never shared his hobby of yoga with anyone. He was a ball bustin' Hood, after all.

But as he watched her through the glass with a screaming newborn in her arms, the smile on her face spoke volumes. Kim was happy. She sat in a glider rocker, put her feet up and brought the baby close to her. She began to talk to the baby, and by the end of the hour, the cries had subsided.

Kim continued to rock him, always stroking his cheek or touching his hand. She was so gentle, her arms wrapped protectively, lovingly around his tiny body. Zach had never seen anything so touching. She caught him looking at her once, and she shocked him by blowing him a kiss.

Zach didn't move, because her attention was drawn back to the baby. She didn't realize she had even done it. Standing on the observation side of the glass, unable to but wanting to disturb Kim in the most provocative way, he was annoyed by his vibrating phone. "Hood."

"You got a cold?" Hugh asked.

"Yeah," Zach told him. "What's up?"

"We've got something. The blood that was on one of the panes of glass produced a hit. We initially couldn't identify it, but it just came back to Lieutenant Franklin."

"Him again. Do I need to pull in Themis?" Zach could feel his anger building. It had been a while since he'd busted some heads. The man had conveniently gone missing. But Zach knew he'd find him eventually.

"Don't pull her in. Her shift is nearly over," Rob said, although Zach hadn't known he was on the call. "We're riding tonight to his old spots. His wife was very helpful today with suggestions."

"Zach, she's probably going to be pulled off that drug case."

He sucked his teeth. "She's not going to be happy about that, but if it's for her safety, that's what counts. If you're riding, I'm going," Zach told them. He needed to burn some energy, and they needed movement on their case.

"Negative," Hugh responded. "We're riding, meeting as planned tonight. But this changes things."

The contentment Kim felt extended until she pulled up to Rob's house. All of the lights were on, and there were cars lining the circular driveway.

"How long are we staying?" Kim asked Zach, who seemed quieter than usual.

"Not long. I know you're tired. We've got to get a few things tied up, and then we can go home."

Kim sighed. "Okay. Good. My back is hurting. I've missed stretching in dance class."

"You miss Clark."

Kim smiled. "I *do* miss Clark," she admitted. "But you're a decent substitute."

"I don't know what you're talking about, but I'm better looking than him." He shook his head getting out of the truck.

The sound of water welcomed them as she followed Zach, who held her hand gently, guiding her through the darkness to the screened-in deck off the lake.

Kim saw Ben and Rob, then their wives. They were gorgeous couples with equally beautiful babies.

Gorgeous women like these two didn't usually gravitate toward women like her. They usually found out she was a judge and had graduated from Yale, and didn't want to have anything to do with a woman who was both smart *and* pretty.

But she, like most of Atlanta, had been sympathetic to LaKota Hood when her attacker, Odesi, had been captured on live TV. It had been an international news story that had made the Hoods even more famous.

"Kim Thurman," she said, introducing herself, prepared for the women to give her a cursory hello and excuse themselves.

"Zoe Hood. Nice to meet you, Judge."

Then Zoe hugged her. Unexpectedly, Kim's apprehension slid away, though she didn't react. She barely managed to stammer, "Pl-please, call me Kim."

"Wow," Zoe said, her eyes wide. "Okay." She sounded thrilled. She touched the other woman, who stood next to her whispering to Rob. "I'd like to introduce you to my best friend and sister-in-law."

The tall woman turned and Kim's breath caught. "Oh, my."

Her easy smile was comforting. "LaKota Hood. This is DaKota."

The healthy baby was in a jumper, attached to her mother's stomach. Black hair swirled around her head, and her head snapped at hearing her name.

"She's quite the busy little girl," her mom said, rubbing her leg. "Quite inquisitive."

"Kim Thurman," Kim said, extending her hand.

LaKota took it, leaned in and touched her cheek to Kim's. "Welcome to our home. Please make yourself comfortable. Would you like some juice?"

Everyone watched LaKota, protective of her. "Yes," Kim said, "that would be lovely."

DaKota gurgled, grabbing some of her mother's long hair. "DaKota," the woman said softly, and spoke to her in the Lakota language. Though the baby was young, she seemed to understand her mother. Eventually, she released her hair, and LaKota went inside for the juice.

Rob and the men watched the exchange.

"What did she say to her?" Hugh asked Rob, who shrugged.

"I don't know. They have this connection that's unbreakable, but DaKota and I have our own language."

"What do you say to her?" Kim asked Rob.

"Does she want to read the sports section first or the business section? She chooses sports every time."

They all laughed, as Rob turned the meat on a gorgeous barbecue grill.

Kim sat on plush patio furniture. She made a mental note to buy furniture for her backyard. This was what a home was supposed to feel like. The only thing missing was Zach by her side. He was with his brother Ben and they were in a deep discussion. She was glad to breathe. Being with Zach was wonderful, but today had been long and she was feeling more like taking him to bed and making love than visiting.

Rob worked the grill like a craftsman and she enjoyed watching. "What's new?" she asked.

"Lieutenant Franklin was the one breaking into your house," Hugh informed her. "His blood was on your window. We're picking him up tonight."

"I'm sure the chief will not be happy."

Rob shook his head. "Definitely not, but he had his chance. We put all the pieces together, so the D.A. will have an ironclad case. He's also the one who tried to kidnap you and Clark."

Kim covered her mouth. "Are you serious?" The shock sent ripples down her spine. She looked around, wondering if they were safe.

"Yes."

"Who was the other guy?"

"Another guard who's in protective custody until we find Franklin."

"Bryson paid him a lot of money to get you. But that's beside the point. I don't want you to get too worried or too comfortable. We still have a long way to go.

We also found out about the woman from the ice cream store," Rob said, trying to slather sauce on the meat.

"What?" Despite what he'd said, the comfort she'd felt was being chased away by anxiety. "What about her?"

"She used an alias to get the job. We have her photo, but not her name. Do you recognize this person?"

Hugh brought the computer over and allowed Kim to take her time looking at the photo. Slowly Kim shook her head. "No. I feel like a witness who saw everything but missed all the important things."

"Don't get discouraged," Zach told her. He'd finally come to sit beside her. When his legs touched hers, electric currents seemed to run up and down her skin. Kim rubbed her knee. When she did it a second time, Zach ran his hand down her leg to her ankle.

"Where does it hurt?"

"Nowhere, I'm fine."

"Okay," Zach said, not touching her for a moment. "We checked the street cameras, and she was crafty in avoiding them. She obviously knew what she was doing. She hasn't been back to work, either."

Hugh snapped his fingers and walked off with the computer. "We just keep looking," he said, typing on the keys. "We found out the truth about Franklin and Daniels, and we will about this woman."

Kim didn't say anything right away, giving their words time to work their way into her.

Ben watched her, then sat beside her. "We discovered Franklin making an attempt to get on your property, and the security we've put into place is working. Ice is sitting on him now."

"Why would Franklin break into my house after all of this? Doesn't he know what's been going on in court?"

"No. He has no more access to Bryson."

"What about other guards? Surely he still has friends on the inside."

Zach put his hand on her back. "Bryson isn't at that jail anymore, so Franklin doesn't know where he's been taken. With no access, Franklin can't help but wonder what's going on. He's burning up the wire trying to find him, but he can't."

"Doesn't he see what his inmates are going through being prisoners? Conspiring to kill a judge is a death sentence."

"Well, he's desperate. He's going to try to complete the job because he wants the money. He's trying to find Bryson to make sure the deal is still on." Hugh tracked the calls, showing Rob the most recent. He took a call from Ice.

"She's got a line on Franklin. He just bought two new untraceable cell phones at a convenience store on Hollowell."

"Why not just pick him up now, and end this?" Kim asked. "He deserves to be in jail and I deserve to be free from all this drama," Kim said calmly.

"Because we want to catch him in the act."

Chapter 12

Zach stood in the shadows, watching Lieutenant Franklin make his way from the gate to the house. The man took his time because he'd done this so many times before. He didn't know this would be his last time.

They'd made a big deal about making it known that the gate had been disabled, and somehow the news had gotten back to Franklin, because he didn't bother with the code. He just unlatched it and walked onto the property.

He seemed to be made of Teflon as he waded through the razorlike bushes to get to the windows, where he spent nearly an hour cutting the glass from its frame.

Zach watched, learning. The man had extraordinary patience.

Once Franklin had made a large enough entry for his slightly overweight body, he pushed his way into the keeping room, and Zach waited, still, until the cop was all the way in before he surprised the man with an uppercut to the jaw. He recovered quickly and hit Zach a few times, but Zach was quicker and got him down. He covered the man's mouth, stepped on his hand, breaking all of the fingers on his right hand.

He muffled the lieutenant's screams with his own leather gloves. Zach pulled him up and came down hard, cracking Franklin's tibia with his knee as he guided the wannabe killer to the floor. "You came to kill her? How about I return the favor?" Gripping the man's neck in a vice grip, he squeezed and heard him gurgling.

Franklin swung with his good arm, his fist whizzing by Zach's chin, just barely clipping his nose. He then reached for his weapon, but Zach beat him to it.

"I've got a cure for idiots like you." He pushed the gun into Franklin's eye, until the man wailed so loudly the sound got on Zach's nerves. "Shut up." Zach hit his radio. "Come get this fool."

The he commanded, "Lights on." The room brightened a bit.

Franklin nursed his hurt leg, murder gleaming from his dark eyes. "You know what, Hood?"

"Don't care, Franklin."

"One day we'll cross paths again. Me and you. Me and your kid. You'll regret knowing me."

Zachary laughed and shook the man's broken hand, causing soprano-quality screams to come from the forty-eight-year-old, as Zach cuffed him behind his back. "I already regret knowing you. You see, Franklin, I don't play fair. Never have, never will. Even if I think it's you and it's not, I'm coming after you. You feel me?"

The remainder of the house was pitch-black, but the alarm finally sounded, and Zach pushed the button on his wrist, silencing it. "The subject has been neutralized. We're in sector one. He's going to need a medic," he reported into his radio.

"I know my rights." Franklin breathed heavily, his size making moving difficult.

Zach dragged him away from the window of the keeping room, letting him bleed on the floor and not the expensive rugs.

"You'd better help me, or I'll make you sorry, Hood!" He used his good leg to kick Zach.

Zach turned around and didn't think twice before using his fist to separate Franklin's front teeth.

"I got rights," he hissed through his new gap.

"What are your rights?" The door was shut tight and the lights Zach had turned on a moment ago were low.

"I have a right to counsel. I have the right to remain silent."

"Then shut the hell up."

"I have a right to not be abused by you."

"Say something else I don't like and you're getting smacked. Simple."

"You can't just beat people up on a burglary charge. That's police abuse. I could sue you."

"I haven't arrested you."

"Fine, then I'm leaving."

"Move and I'll break your other leg."

Franklin used his good foot to scoot himself backward. "Don't!"

"Why are you here? Why are you trying to kill the judge?"

"She's worth a lot of money in the joint. A lot of people are willing to pay good money to see her dead. We get furloughed because the city can't pay us and I have to work for free while she works on her golf swing. That's bullshit."

Zach had to admit the man had a point, but that wasn't Kim's fault. "She didn't make the rules. You need to take your concerns to your union rep."

"I'd rather see her dead and get her paycheck. Then she insults the police department and hires you. Instead of standing up for us cops, she's hires a bunch of Hood gangsters. You ain't better than us. You just got more money and brothers who saved your ass so you wouldn't be me." The man swore, letting the blood dribble down his face to his arm.

The lights came on in the hallway, then brighter in the keeping room. Ice slid in low, a cannon in her hand, followed by Ben, holding his 9 mm Glock. "Excellent catch," she said to Zach, noting Franklin's broken state. "He's alive."

"Where you taking me, bitch?" Franklin asked Ice.

"I've never heard that before. Come on, Mr. Original," she said, checking his wounds. Ice signed to Zach that Kim was at the top of the stairs, but she'd backed into the darkness so nobody else could see her. "I've had my nursing degree for ten years, but there's nothing saying I've got to use it. And I'm not the cops. I ain't got to be nice to you. I'm gon' fix you up in my back-yard, then take you to jail." She put a stabilizing brace on his leg, and she and Ben helped him stand.

Franklin looked scared. "I shoulda left that woman alone the minute I saw you Hoods. You fools are crazy! I know one thing. You hurt me," he said to Ice, "and I'll come after you and make a real woman outta you!"

"You know, I love potholes," she told him. "I'm going to hit every one of them on the way to the hospital." He squealed in pain, tears streaming from his eyes.

"Smile for the camera," Ben told him, pulling the concealed camera from the shelf and showing Franklin the movie of him breaking in. "I'll make sure this and your confession are played on every news station tomorrow as the first story."

The cop cursed until he was out of breath, and Ben kept taping until Ice him pulled away. Once she pulled through the gate, two cars fell in behind her to trail her to the hospital.

"How's Themis?" Ben asked, referring to Kim.

"I'm fine," she said from upstairs. Neither of them had seen or heard her, but Ice had. Zach was surprised. Usually he knew exactly when she was awake. He went to the bottom of the stairs and looked up. He caught a glimpse of the bottom of her gown.

"I'm glad you're fine," Ben said. "I'm going back to work. Zach, you're off duty. We've got eight agents in the neighborhood. Get a good night's sleep. You, too, Kim."

"I will. Good night."

Zach hugged his brother and locked the door behind

him. He secured the keeping room window and the door, and headed into the guest room, where he'd planned to sleep for the night.

Tired, he pulled off his clothes and got into the shower, his body weary after nearly three weeks of around-the-clock surveillance. Tonight was the culmination of a group effort and they'd been successful. The reward: sleep. He washed his hair and cleaned his ears. Pulling off the towel, he lathered on lotion and left the bathroom.

The room was jet-black, just the way he liked it. Sliding beneath the Egyptian cotton sheets, he nearly jumped out of bed when Kim's body touched his.

"What the hell?" he asked.

"I didn't mean to scare you. I'll stay on my side of the bed." She scooted over, rumpling the covers as she moved.

Zach laughed, his body revived, the weariness gone. "That's my side."

Kim kicked her long silk gown and moved closer to him. "I'll switch with you."

"This is my side, too."

"Oh," she said.

"Lady, what are you doing here?"

"I don't want to sleep by myself." Her barely covered breast was touching his arm. "I'll stay out of your way, Zach. I promise."

"Stay out of my way in a bed the size of a sliding glass door? That's impossible, and not something I want at all."

"Oh."

"You didn't think that," he told her. "You couldn't have thought that when you walked down those stairs."

"No, I didn't think that. Worst case, I thought you'd let me sleep here. Best case, you'd make love to me and let me sleep here."

"Whoa. Wow." In the dark, his hands found hers and Zach moved on top of her. "There are no six-lane highways with you, are there?"

"No. I say what I mean. Saves time." Kim sighed when his thigh moved hers apart and settled between her legs. The pressure from her legs felt wonderful. She smelled faintly of warmth and lotion and mouthwash.

"Take this off," he said of her gown. Sliding it up from her thighs, he cupped her legs, kissing them as he moved higher, the silk cool against the places he'd made hot.

Her hands were gentle against his skin, something he had missed. Her feminine touch, comforting. Zach had been waiting for the right woman for so long, been wanting Kim for so long; now that he had her in his arms, he didn't want to let go.

Her breasts were full and sensitive as he claimed them. Her breathless response made him desire her more. He licked her nipples and she arched, holding his head, her legs wrapping his. All of her body seemed to blossom and he wanted her. Just as they had an understanding when she left court, they had one now. He wanted her to be more than satisfied, but he didn't want to rush. He wanted to savor all that was her. This was a night to remember.

"Don't slow down," she urged, her voice heavy.

"Sex is like good food. You don't want to eat too fast."

"Eat," she said, her hands seeking his sex. "You can always have more."

Kim climbed on top of him and he wished right then he could see her better in the dark. Her attitude turned his desire to passion and he knew his existence teetered on something more than a chance meeting or one physical, sexual experience.

Their worlds had met for an important reason. He tried to stay in the moment, but his brain was taking him a year ahead, five years ahead and even further.

He pushed the thoughts aside, knowing they'd come again, and he cupped her large breasts and savored the taste of her. He'd seen her enough to know what she looked like unclothed, but he vowed he'd never make love to her in the dark again. He would enjoy her this time through his other senses.

She used a cream lotion that kept her skin soft, but it was odorless. Running his tongue along her skin, he suckled her nipples and was rewarded with a yearning sigh, and her hand moved over his head and down the center of his back.

She tasted slightly of warm sugar. He thought of hot chocolate and how delicious it was in the winter. Her foot caressed his leg and he groaned, loving that old feeling. He suckled her again. He was very fond of that delicacy, warm sugar. He sampled the side of her breast and the inside of her arm. He kissed each of her fingers and played hide-and-seek with her thumb in his mouth.

"Zach. Oh!" He thought she was going to orgasm. His name had never sounded better.

Kim giggled when he stopped. "Zachary?" She pried his lips apart and he licked her fingers and the palm of her hand. "That feels amazing," she told him. "You could do this to me every day and I'd never get tired of it."

"Every day?" he double-checked. "It wouldn't get old?"

Her damp arm caressed his cheek as she reached up to hug him. "No, I like it. Like bacon."

He shared a laugh with her, and her breasts moved against his chest. When she giggled, he knew he would never get tired of that. "Enjoy it," he told her and kept up the assault.

He held her foot hostage, kissing her arch and toes, her ankle and behind her knee. She jumped and sucked in breathlessly. His fingers sought her center long before his lips settled there, and she flexed her toes but didn't stop him until her climax spiraled completely out of her body.

Zach didn't wait for her to finish; he wanted to feel her clasp him, and he did. First the ring of her center, then her legs around his back, then her arms around his neck. She was all his. His arms around her, his mind and hers aligned, they were one.

Into the night, he would reach for her and she would be there, until his body's clock shut down for sleep. He had to rest.

They awakened late, both hurrying, rushing through

the kitchen to get coffee, when Hugh called. "We're walking out now. Themis is fifteen minutes behind."

"No need to go in. There was a suspicious package delivery at the courthouse. It's closed for the day. Everyone is working from home. Guess you got a free day."

Zach rubbed his chin, eyeing Kim over the computer screen. "What are you looking at like that?" Hugh asked. "You look like you won a bunch of money. You're not gambling again, are you?"

Kim was behind the computer, doing a striptease. Her very businesslike suit was on the floor. She had on a matching black-and-pink bra-and-panty set. He loved matching underwear.

"Hell, no, I'm not gambling. I haven't gambled since I was sixteen and we went to Six Flags. I've got to go. You might as well take today off. I'll have Rob relieve you. You can get out and run whatever errands you need to. I'm sure you probably need a break."

"I'm fine. Later." Zach closed the computer. He took off his watch and radio, and set the time for one hour. He'd sign in then and see if there was anything going on. They could always call him if they needed to contact him, but right now he needed some private time with Kim.

"So you're a gambler?" she asked, backing up in her stilettos.

"I was. Now I only bet on sure things. Like, right now, I bet I'm going to make love to you."

Her smile was quick. She suppressed a giggle and her eyebrow shot up. "Are you sure about that?"

She held up the ugly skirt to the ugly suit she'd been

wearing. Before she could fix her mouth to say anything, he'd tossed the skirt far away. Kim screamed,
laughing. In her heels, she ran to his room and was
nearly to the bed when he caught her. He swept her into
his arms and spun her around.

"Zach!" She giggled. "I'm dizzy." She laughed.

"That's the way I like 'em. Dizzy for me."

He spun her around, but she'd stopped laughing. He
looked at her face to see if she was all right. "What?"

Like a newborn calf, she wobbled to the bed and sat,
brushing her hair from her eyes. "But I'm not stupid. If
you like dumb girls, I'm not the one."

"Don't you think I know that? The question is, why
do you want to be with me? Because I'm convenient?"

She shook her head and her curls bounced around her
face. She looked innocent and sad. "Despite my profession, you like me. You don't need me to make you."

Zach understood more than she knew. He had money,
and after big cases, Hood Investigations got a lot attention; he, being single, was the bearer of a lot of it.
But he needed a woman who was genuine. The judge,
sitting on his bed in her bra, panties and stilettos, was
looking pretty authentic.

"I'm thinking one of us is overdressed."

Kim made a big deal of looking down at herself, then
at him. "I've got on two things, and you, well…a lot."

"What about the shoes? That's more than two."

She scooted back on the bed and lay back, crossing
her legs in the air. "I think I'll keep the shoes and get
rid of everything else."

Zach was undressed in seconds and she still beat him

to getting naked. The panties and bra had little Velcro sides. Progress amazed him. When she started at the bottom of his body and worked her way up, he thought he'd burst all over her, but Kim was an expert at controlling him as she was herself.

When he finally claimed her, her voice was hoarse. His was, too. He spent himself, wanting to memorize the feel of her coming with him inside of her. He curled around her back, listening to her breathing as she fell asleep, his body sliding from exertion, to relaxation, to sleep.

The chopper noise from overhead really didn't bother him. Hood Investigations had found out only that they could be from a magazine that was investigating judges. Beyond that, no further information was forthcoming. Hood had accepted Kim's explanation about her ex-boyfriend and his effort to become a reality TV star, and Hood had been very careful in their research, not wanting to fuel that fire. That would be all he needed to realize his dream. But so far, even that hadn't panned out.

Zach had to know. He was more vested than ever in keeping her safe. He liked her. More than that… He liked her a lot. His eyes closed. There was a scratching sound, but it was drowned out by the sound of the beating chopper blades and Kim's even breathing. He would do the work required to get the answers needed, and he'd get them today.

Sleep dragged him under.

Chapter 13

"I want Judge Thurman dead. Smoke the witch. Take care of it."

The unmistakable sound of the defendant's voice was heard on the wiretap, along with the lieutenant agreeing to the terms and when it was supposed to happen and how.

Kim listened along with the entire Hood team, the chief of police and the prosecutor, defense and District Attorney.

"Gentlemen, what's our plan of action?" she asked.

"The lieutenant confessed and he's taking a plea to spare his family a public trial," the chief said. "Judge Thurman, I apologize for any discomfort I may have caused you."

The room remained silent. "I realize you were working with the best information possible. Thank you for your effort, Chief." Kim stood and shook his hand.

"We will be holding a press conference at noon. We would like you to attend."

"I won't be making any statements, but I'm sure you will do a fine job," she said. "Rob, please show the chief out."

Dismissed, the chief left the room without being able to be the real hero of the hour.

The District Attorney and the defense attorney, Phinney, stepped forward. "The offer is life without the possibility of parole," Phinney offered. "Mr. Bryson will have to secure new counsel for the case against you."

Kim regarded the attorney. "I'm shocked you're not asking for a mistrial." Defeat didn't become Phinney. He normally fought for everything.

"I strongly recommended it, but my client refused to listen."

Kim shook her head. "No. I'm granting a mistrial. Let another judge hear this case with all the evidence."

The District Attorney reacted. "You realize you could be called as a witness."

Kim nodded. "I know. But I don't want Bryson to have immediate grounds for appeal by taking this plea. This case is declared a mistrial. I will dismiss the jury. Thank you, gentlemen."

Watching the defense attorney's defeated posture, Kim saw that the plea suggestion had been a strategy to keep his client off death row, and that she'd made the right decision. They left quietly, leaving the Hood men in her office. "What is it?" Kim asked.

"The woman from the ice cream store is still unexplained."

All of the Hoods looked displeased about this.

"Zach, you don't have any evidence that there is anyone else," Hugh countered. "We could have scared that woman underground. Maybe she's a girlfriend of Franklin's. The one he was giving his wife's money to. Maybe she was a random angry woman who was just pissed off at Kim, and maybe she'll never commit another crime again."

"Hugh, I heard scratching on the roof of the house last night, and that helicopter keeps me up. There are unexplained occurrences, and we have to find out what's going on."

Hugh chuckled as if Zach was challenging his science.

"You heard some scratching on the house? That was probably branches from the trees. Besides, we investigated and didn't find anything."

"We base cases on assumption all the time. We did when Ben believed somebody was robbing Zoe's store, and we had no proof. We didn't see anybody entering or exiting Zoe's Diamonds. I'll do it myself if I have to."

Rob and Ben shook their heads. "We've been there," they said in unison. "You're not going it alone. We're going to stick with you. Kim, if he believes there's something there, we do, too."

"Thank you," she said, relieved. They weren't like the police chief. Abandoning her because the cameras were gone. "I have to go back to court and dismiss the jury. Zach, can I see you for a moment, please?"

Everyone else filed out, and Kim met Zach in the center of the room, her hands outstretched. "I appreciate you not giving up. I can't imagine being in the house alone and someone attacking me."

"No one's going to do anything to you. I'm Zach Hood, you know. I'm made of carbonized steel, so you're safe from all threats."

Kim giggled, then hesitated, stroking his ego. "Okay. What's carbonized steel?"

He pretended to spank her, then ended by caressing her butt and thighs. "Girl, don't make me remind you." His hand met a rough surface. "What's that?"

"My gun holster."

"What?" Zach was serious now, his hands between her legs, removing the .38 snub-nosed revolver. "Why?"

"I won't be one of those judges whose life depends on someone else. When you taught that self-defense class, I realized it was important to think past one day. I had to think about being careful all of my life. If that includes carrying a gun, then so be it. As you can see, I can't trust the people whose job it is to protect me. If today was going to be your last day, I wanted to be prepared in more ways than one."

Zach looked as if he was reading her. Like he could see into her soul. He didn't know she didn't have one. She'd cried it out over her parents' graves.

He cupped her neck and kissed her forehead before looking into her eyes. "That's not what you think. You want to insulate yourself from getting hurt. You think

I'm leaving you, and this is how I'd do it, in this public way, when I wouldn't."

Kim didn't try to pull away or deny his statement. "Of course I did. That's what people do. No one tells the truth at the end of a relationship. They say they'll call and they don't. They just stop calling. You're left to wonder what happened, and after a few days you know you're the fool for not realizing earlier that it's over. Or, they say and do hurtful things to one another."

Zach wanted to kiss the words from her mouth, but he let her finish. "That's not necessary between us. We had something special, and I don't want to mess it up by being overly emotional, or thinking it could be more than it was."

"So you're putting Zach Hood to the curb? Is that what's happening here?"

She caressed his jaw. She loved how tall he was and how he had to look straight down when she was next to him to see into her eyes. "Yes."

"No," he countered quickly.

She couldn't help smiling at him. "Zach, what are you saying?"

"Lady, you're not getting rid of me. We've got a criminal to catch."

She reached up and he kissed her palm. Despite knowing that crying didn't help anything, tears filled her eyes, but she didn't let them fall.

"You know, Kim, all I can think about is making passionate love to you. I want to feed you and hear you laugh. I want to take you to my brother's house and watch you sit on a blanket and play with DaKota. I want to be with you when you're afraid. I want to watch you sleep."

She pressed her lips to his because his eyes said so much more that she couldn't hear.

He wanted her to fall in love with him the way he was falling in love with her.

He swore and she looked at him, her green-and-blue stilettos peeking from beneath her black robe. "We'll see, baby. In time. We'll see."

"Go to work and let me do my job." He kissed her fingers, knowing her now and how much she loved having them licked and sucked. The intimacy of what they were doing was unbelievably tender, especially since they were surrounded by volumes of books, where one side had been decided against.

Passion encircled them. She brought his head down and her mouth met his in a kiss of lovers, hungry for one another. Their bodies swayed in a steady motion.

"Can I keep my gun?" she asked when they separated.

"No," he said, as he knelt down and caressed her thigh. His hand found the curve of her bottom and she ran her hand over his head, looking at him tenderly. They were meant to be together. How could she think of cutting him off? Zach finally holstered her gun. "Yes. Do not ever let me see this unless I'm dead."

Her arms encircled his back and she squeezed him hard. "Don't say that. Don't ever say that, Zachary."

"Baby, I was joking." He stood and was caught in an embrace so fierce. "I was kidding. I'm sorry."

"Don't!" He heard the catch in her voice. "You have all those Hoods who care about you. You have people

to leave your money to. I'm alone. I care about you."
She backed away from him. "I'm allergic to cats, but
I'm leaving my money to cats. Don't joke about dying."

His apologetic smile broke her heart. "I won't. Let
me walk with you."

"No." She shook her head. "I need to pull myself
together. I've got to dismiss the jury and then I've got
a sentencing hearing in Courtroom A. Twenty-four-
year-old killed a family in a car crash. Let Rob take me
today."

"I'm going to be in your courtroom in a half hour. I
can come now."

"I know. In a half hour, I'll be ready for you then."
She winked and blew him a kiss. "See you later, handsome."

"Damn," he swore appreciatively. "I can't wait."

She disappeared through the door, and when Rob
stuck his head in to acknowledge acceptance of
Themis—the judge and the Greek goddess of law—
Zach gave him the thumbs-up.

"That woman is going to be the death of me," Zach
murmured, rubbing his eyes.

"No, she won't, but next time turn off your radio so
I don't want to kill you," Hugh told him via radio. His
dry spell of having no love had lasted so long, he had
commented more than once that he now qualified to be
a part-time monk.

Zach's bark of laughter shot through the radio and
into Hugh's earpiece. "You're jealous, and that's not
pretty."

"Damn straight, homie."

* * *

Zach wanted Kim's body *and* her mind. She was so focused on her caseload, she'd forgotten to eat. He'd begun bringing her lunch at her desk, and she was so touched by the gesture that no matter the food he brought her, she made him feel happy to do it. Then she would insist they eat together. Soon, she had him watching dancing shows that she'd saved on her DVR. She would get really close to the TV and study the technique of the dancer, then come back to the couch and sit next to Zach, telling him, "I can do that. I'm a better dancer than she is."

He'd laugh and challenge her, and then she'd get up, put on her stilettos and show him how good she really was.

The truth was, he liked to see the judge dancing for him in her office between cases. Her life was so serious, every second so full of everyone else's tragedies, that when she had a moment to smile or put on her silly face, he wanted to see it. He was going to save her life. He'd promised her that last night, and she'd assured him, in the sparkling twilight of the full moon, that she believed him.

Today he'd taken the day to think, but he needed to be with Kim. He couldn't not see her for a whole day.

Zach sat in his office at his work space, a comfortable leather sofa that partially overlooked the gardens of the other office building on the lot, and the complex gym. The best part was that it was the women's workout area, where they lifted weights. At any time of the day or night, women were squatting, bending or pumping some part of their body all for their—and his—enjoyment.

Today he couldn't focus on tight buns, for the note in his hand. He'd read it a hundred times. This was the one mystery he hadn't been able to solve. The message was articulate, but simple. *You will feel my pain.* It was so TV, he thought. So dramatic. No man would write this. Unless he wrote for television.

He reached for his beer, pen and pad. He scribbled *female* on the paper and circled it. TV writer. Disgruntled employee. But they'd checked everyone. All of the staff had checked out. They'd all expressed regret for having left Kim's employ. Even the recently departed Trevor. Seemed his new job with a Supreme Court justice was less about law and more about being his servant. Kim had treated him with respect, according to Trevor, and he wanted back in.

But even after having been gone only a few days, Zach wasn't sure the judge would have him back. Zach was opposed to the idea until her case was solved. No new variables needed to be introduced until everything else outstanding was settled.

He missed her, he realized. They'd been apart all morning. He was meeting her this afternoon to take her grocery and foundation shopping. He had no idea what the hell foundations were, but he would find out today.

His office door opened and he looked up. "Surprise," Kim said, sticking her head in.

"Hey, what are you doing here?" Thrilled to see her, Zach stood and walked to the door. He took her hand, closing the door as soon as she was inside. "You all right?"

"Yes, baby, I'm fine. My court reporter has the stomach flu, so we closed early for the day. I thought you and I could talk about some things."

She looked at the note. "I'm glad to see that." Kim sat on the couch where Zach had been sitting. "It's cozy in here." Turning to look out the picture window, she could see directly into the gym. "You're such a man."

Zach laughed, rubbing his abs. "Isn't God amazing the way he constructed the woman's body? I'm giving him a fist bump for that."

Kim fell over laughing. "You are ridiculous. A fist bump? I seriously don't think so."

She crossed her legs and the split skirt she was wearing slid open. Zach had no choice but to pay attention. "I was focusing on my work, not really looking at those women. Really, Kim. I had some thoughts on this note," he told her, picking up the paper.

"I did, too." Kim patted the space beside her. "Or would this seat be better?" she said, referring to his well-worn space on the couch with the front-row view of the gym.

Zach sat next to Kim, and before she knew what was happening, he had her on his lap. She squealed, but his lips were against hers in a kiss so hungry, he thought he might have hurt her. He tried to pull away, but her arms went around his neck, and she held on to him. "You'd better not start something and not finish," she whispered.

"I wouldn't think of it."

He pulled the pins from her hair and pitched them onto the floor. "Zachary," she protested lightly. "I need those for later."

"Too bad," he said, as he pulled the last one from the bun, then unwound it and let the soft strands of hair spiral into his palm. Kim let her head fall back and he drove his fingers through her hair from her scalp all the way to the soft ends. She purred and he bit her neck. Kim dissolved in his arms, curling into him.

"You're going to make me be very bad, Zach," she said, her mouth against his neck, where she licked him.

"Baby, sometimes bad is good."

He pushed her skirt up and she scooted forward until their sexes met. "Zach, now, you have to be the grown-up here."

He massaged her thighs, his hands inching higher. "And what are you going to do?"

"You're using your influence over me, and now I have no self-control."

"You're a member of the court," he said, kissing her chest, loving the taste of her. "Self-control is the hallmark of all that you stand for."

"You would think so," she said, pulling down his zipper and freeing his sex, while he pulled up her skirt and moved her thong. They joined and each exhaled sharply.

"So good," she whispered. "I should be disbarred. I have no defense." He pulled her butt, bringing her closer, making her grind her sex against his. "I could do this forever."

Zach couldn't speak anymore. All he could think

about was having her. Their bodies met and separated, met and separated, her pulse beating at her throat. He wanted to claim every bit of her. He was wet with perspiration, and she was wet, too, her hair damp across her face, her sex sliding against his. She was completely beautiful in her silk and pearls on top, her skirt bunched and disheveled at her waist. He couldn't help wanting Kim. He'd never wanted anyone more. "I want you," he told her, holding her close, their tempo controlled by his hands.

He was barely moving inside of her. Their eyes met. "Take me," she growled.

He claimed her mouth hard, their bodies meeting in a frantic coupling that needed no name. Kim pushed up on her knees, but Zach brought her back down onto him, filling her completely, until she squeezed his shoulders with her hands and grit her teeth, coming. Her hair slid down her back and her pulse beat rapidly at her neck. Zach brought her forward, burying his face between her silk-covered breasts, claiming her body until he, too, felt release.

They held tight to one another, their passion easing. "I came here for a reason," Kim said, her face on Zach's shoulder.

"I'm doing the best I can," he joked, enjoying her giggle. "I had something to tell you," he said.

"It might be a woman," they said in unison.

Kim sat up enough to look at him. "The note," they said again, together.

"Finish," Kim told him. "You comfortable?" she asked.

"Could stay this way forever. The note sounds dramatic. In some ways like a woman," Zach pointed out. "I was going to look into the television angle. But I'm not a movie watcher. It's going to take some time to figure this out."

"I appreciate that."

"Why'd you think it was a woman?" he asked.

"Because we've been thinking it's a man. We've caught the men, and this note thing is still out there. The deputies had immediate access to me and my house. I think it was just a matter of time before they hurt me—killed me. We're still missing something."

"Up." He held her waist as she slowly got off his lap and onto her feet.

"Are we disgusting?" she asked, as he held her hand and walked her to his private bathroom.

"Hell, no. We're the people others are jealous of."

Zach left her alone to clean up, then took a few minutes to pull himself back together. When they were finished, they were again a professional couple.

"Let's go over everything. Tell me about the helicopter. How long has it been there?"

"Five annoying weeks. Varying times of the day and night, but they seem to come when I get home and when I'm trying to relax. I've seen those exposé shows on judges and assumed they were there filming me about my work hours. But my hours are logged with the court system. I put in the requisite amount, so I don't understand why they're there. I've tried to find out and I asked the police to investigate. They told me they didn't have enough man hours at the time and would get to it."

Zach called Hugh. "We need to get a bird in the sky and have that helicopter outside Kim's house brought down."

"Done," Hugh said and ended the call.

Kim looked from side to side. "That's it?"

"That's how we roll, baby." He pulled up his jeans and walked around the office, until she couldn't keep her laughter inside. "Hoods can't reveal our secrets. The less you know, the better. We'll find out what we need to know, and when we get the right information we'll call you. If we need your help you can call your Crawford boys."

"Are you really jealous of them?"

"Zachary Hood is jealous of no man, especially the Crawfords, whose butts we kicked in football and basketball back in the day."

"Sounds like that rivalry needs to have stayed there."

"We'll meet those clowns again and when we do, you'll know why we are the champions."

Zach hit the CD player and Jazmine Sullivan started singing. He took Kim's hand and she danced with him, doing a scaled-down samba, while he did an easy side-to-side step. "Zach, you can dance!"

"Shh. My mother made me take lessons. I loved dancing with her, but I don't dance anymore. Side-to-side is good enough for me."

"No," Kim said, looking at his hips. "You have talent. I love dancing. It's so much fun. What do you do for fun, Zach?"

"I read. Play with my nieces. Now I have a nephew.

...an expert marksman." He turned away, embarrassed ...alking about himself.

"No, don't turn away. What about traveling? What haven't you seen? Where would you love to go?"

Kim's sugar-brown eyes were warm with interest. He'd just acted out one of his fantasies: making love to her in his office. And now he was dancing with her and talking about himself. He'd definitely crossed the line on professional. That boat had sailed long ago.

"Tell me, Zach."

"You tell me," he said, spinning her.

"I've been all over Europe," she said in German.

"I'm not as good speaking German," he said in German. "But I've been to France, England and Spain," he said in French. "I want to go to Africa. I've not been in a long time. Cape Town, Johannesburg, South Africa, specifically."

"I've not been to the Caribbean," she said in Spanish.

Zach kissed her nose. "You're kidding. Everyone has been to Aruba, St. John and St. Thomas."

Kim shook her head. "I haven't. I spent a long time—" she hesitated "—in school."

"It's time you told me whatever it is you're not telling me."

"There's nothing to tell."

"Sure there is. Who is your father? You never talk about him. Do you hate his guts?"

"No, I never could hate a man I didn't really know."

"So he wasn't there?"

"No. I've said enough." Kim tried to pull away, but Zach wouldn't let her go. "Let me go."

"What just happened?" Her posture had changed, her eyes were different. Even her hands were stiff. "Kim, talk to me. What just happened?"

"Nothing. I've got to go back to work."

"Work's over for today. Tell me the truth. What are you hiding?"

In her eyes were storm clouds, and he knew he was about to get blasted. "Nothing! Get out of my business! Save my life. That's what I'm paying you to do."

She pulled, and this time he let her go. "You're keeping their secrets and they're dead. What good is that doing you? Huh? She has a room, but no pictures of you. He didn't even have a room. They shipped you across the world to go to school, blacked out your life, and you're here all by yourself. Kim, what is it?"

"I'm not a Hood! I'm not you! I don't have brothers and sisters and cousins and houses and more love than I know what to do with. Nobody loves me, okay, Zach? It's not the end of the world."

"You're such a great person." She shook her head and he knew those weren't the right words to say.

"Don't go there. I'm a great gal. Great potential," she said, giving herself the thumbs-up. "I've heard it all. I know that. I'm a judge. I've exceeded all expectations. I'm going to be just fine."

She turned on her heels, trying to get to the door, and he reached for her, but she threw up her hands. "I'm all right." She pulled her jacket tight around her waist. "Just save my life, Zach. That's all I'm asking."

"Kim, where are you going?"

She wasn't crying and Zach didn't understand. He felt as if his heart was being ripped out. "I'm going to the lobby. I can't leave without someone taking me. I know how to obey rules, so I'll wait out there."

"I'll take you."

Her nod was stilted. She pulled her hair back, braided it, wrapped the braid and tucked the end at the nape of her neck into her bun. She was the judge again. Zach admired her self-control, but he also knew every pressure cooker would blow. He just wondered when Kim's time would come.

Chapter 14

Sleep didn't come for hours, so she drank, hoping that would help. When it didn't, she put on her sneakers and got on her treadmill, only to find out liquor and exercise didn't go together.

Showering and pulling on silk lounging pants and a sweatshirt, Kim decided to confront her past. Her hands full of garbage bags and a sixteen-ounce glass of Grey Goose and juice, she opened the door to the keeping room and walked inside.

"Mum," she said, speaking in German to her mother's picture over the fireplace. Kay had insisted she only speak German, the language of the Swiss where she'd sent her daughter to school. "It's time I did a little spring cleaning." Kim laughed. "I know. It's the end of October. I guess a little fall cleaning never hurt anyone.

Mum, I've had a lot of questions about love. Can you tell me what it is?"

Kim sat on the sofa and looked up at the painting of her and her mother. "I know it's that god-awful heaviness in your chest when you feel like you're running and skipping. But why does it make you act so stupid?"

Kim drank from her glass and waited. "You're going to have to speak up. I can't hear you, Mum. Right, it's complicated. You have a PhD in sociology, and that's what you tell me. No wonder I've never had a real boyfriend. Give me more, Dr. Thurman. I am very jealous of this man I like, Mum. He's very handsome and he has brothers and sisters. I wonder why you and Dad never gave me siblings. Didn't I deserve to be happy? You two had each other. You spied on people, tore apart lives, invaded their privacy—all for your country, and you left me alone with no one. So I meet someone, Mum, and I pulled a Herbert Thurman.

"I lashed out at him for being a good guy with a family. Kay Thurman, you and Herbert have made a mess of me, making me keep your secrets. I need siblings, Kay, darling."

Her voice caught and she pushed on the fireplace, turning the poker. "Tell Herbert it's okay if he cheated, if only to give me a sister so I can have someone to talk to."

Kim drained her glass and set it on the floor. Opening the garbage bag, she scooped the contents off the coffee table into the bag, then moved to the desk.

"Herbert, you loyal bastard. I've needed a brother or sister, but you only made me. I'm so sad…and lonely."

She took a key off the desk and went back to the fireplace. Using all her mental faculties to focus, she inserted the key in the fireplace and turned it.

Zach counted to thirty, waiting for Kim to come out of the secret room. He'd not seen it on any blueprints of the house, but knowing now what he did, he understood why. Kim wasn't talking or crying or anything. That concerned him. He moved quietly into the keeping room, when he saw her with her arms full.

"Hey, love," she said, her eyes bleary, her speech slurred and German. "I was thinking—garage sale. But I can't carry all these glasses."

"English, please."

She giggled. "Right. My father loved collecting glasses. But these are heavy."

"They're solid gold."

"So they are," she said. "I should donate the money to the children's ward at the hospital."

She swayed back into the room, her hips moving invitingly. "This was Herbert's room. They couldn't be separated, he and Kay. He was a lovely man, Zach. You would have loved him. He engaged manly men. He hardly talked to me when I was home, but I enjoyed listening to him when he talked."

Zach put his arm around her waist and tried to guide her out of the hallway leading to her father's room. Honestly, he felt uncomfortable, first for not knowing about the room, but also not knowing if it was secure or not.

Zach was pleasantly surprised that it was so modern and had electrical power. He had to report this to Hugh immediately, so he discreetly took pictures, as Kim pointed out paintings Zach recognized.

"Herbert loved collecting Renoir. They were spies, Zach. All the things people think and imagine about spies are false. They don't slink about in trench coats. They fit into your environment." She yawned. "I'm taking the keeping room apart, Zach. It will be no more."

"We'll see how you feel in the morning."

"I'll feel the same way as I do now. My mind is made up. I'm so tired." Kim walked out of the room, a cup in her hands, pushing hair behind her ears. "Good night, Herbert." She stared up at her mother. "Kay, I wish you loved me more. Good night, Mum," she said in German. She put the cup down and left the room, closing the door behind herself.

"Zach, can I sleep with you tonight, even though I was so mean to you earlier? You have every right to say no, for me to go to my own room and be a baby bitch there."

Zach chuckled, taking her hand and guiding her to his room. He held up the covers and waved her in.

Kim got in, her hair covering her face. She wiped it off. "Come here," she said.

"You're in no shape to make love," he told her, sliding into his warm bed.

Zach slid into her welcoming embrace and stroked her back. "Terrorism isn't new, Zach. Kay and Herbert were killed by terrorists who discovered they were spies. I was schooled in Switzerland so I wouldn't be killed, too. I was Raquel Wheeler, but I am Kimberly

Thurman. They didn't love me too closely because they didn't want to lose me."

"That means they loved you tremendously, baby."

"I wish they'd loved me more." Her breathing evened and she sniffed.

She'd turned on the heat in the house. This was the first night the temperature had dipped into the thirties. The heat hissed on. Kim crawled onto Zach's side of the bed and turned around, nestling her butt in his groin. "I love you, baby," she said, bringing his arm around to cover her.

He kissed her beautiful hair. "I love you, too."

He fell asleep, knowing there was nothing more perfect than this.

Kim saw the remnants of her episode when she took her first steps toward the kitchen to find coffee. "What a mess," she said aloud.

"Sure enough." Flora moved the gold cups with great care onto the kitchen table.

Kim jumped, her heart in her throat. "I wasn't expecting you today."

"That's obvious." The sixty-eight-year-old woman had been a member of the household since before Kim was born. She slid the bucket of soapy water out of the way by the kitchen door. "Trevor called. He said he doesn't like his job with the justice and wants to come back."

"He should have thought of that when he quit and didn't give notice."

"I'll tell you when I'm quitting. You'll see my dead body in my Cadillac on the driveway."

Kim chuckled. "Hush, Flora. You've been saying that for years. How's that old Ford holding up? And Fords are not Cadillacs, you know."

The older woman squirted some cleaner on the cabinet and wiped it down, along with the door handles. "It's holding up better than you, that's for sure."

"Please, Flora. Tell me how you feel before I have my coffee. You must not like having a job."

"You've fired me thirty times in the last thirty years. I haven't gone anywhere yet. Zach is cute. I think we should marry him."

Kim scalded her lip on her first sip of coffee. "What? I can barely get a good night's sleep and you're talking marriage? Please go wash something—not in this kitchen."

"Sure, treat me like the maid."

Kim sat at the kitchen table and crossed her legs, drinking her coffee. "You *are* the maid, lady. Gracious." Kim remembered a time when Flora was quiet—when her parents were alive.

"Flora, you sexy chica," Zach said to the woman as he entered the kitchen. He put his arm around her shoulder and kissed her cheek. Flora beamed with flirtatious pride.

Kim wanted to throw something at all their good cheer. "Tell me how you two met?"

"He was checking my background, and I invited him to check out all of me," the old woman cackled with ill-concealed glee. "He wanted to, but he was on the job.

I told him I don't mind bending the rules about sleeping with the help. Baby, bring it on." Flora snapped her fingers in the air and shook her hips from side to side. She'd been with Kim so long, Kim couldn't start correcting her now. She could hardly fire her. Flora had been her nanny when she was a little girl.

"You are fired," Kim said, trying not to smile as she sipped her coffee. "I mean it this time. I promise."

Ignoring her once-small charge, Flora wiped down more counters as she talked. "You tore that room up, Ms. Kim. Am I fired before or after I clean it up?" She winked at Zach.

"After, of course. And after the groceries. Well, you're on probation."

"I need a raise, come to think of it." Flora took the gold cups with her as she left the kitchen. "A lady stopped by, asking, did you need some household help? I told her no, she better get off this property or I'd bust a cap in her behind. I figured she got to the door 'cause I left the gate open. I hadn't."

"Flora!"

"You don't have to scream. I'm in the hallway."

"When did this happen?" Kim asked, meeting Flora in the beautiful foyer, where she was mopping.

"An hour ago."

Zach called Hugh, and the team was there in minutes. Hugh had Flora cornered so he could draw a picture of the woman. The composite was of the woman from the ice cream store. They fingerprinted the door and got one.

Zach promised Flora a nice vacation, and she did the

happy dance all the way up the stairs to clean Kim's bathroom.

"You have a cast of characters working for you," Zach told her as he made some tea, the team leaving as quickly as they came. He joined Kim at the window as she sipped her second cup of coffee. "In the spring, beautiful goldfinch birds will come into these trees. They're very pretty. You'll also get the redbreast robins and cardinals."

"Wouldn't you rather talk about Herbert and Kay?"

He didn't miss a beat. "Yes."

"What do you want to know?"

"Who were they working for?"

"I don't know. Likely the CIA and a man named Paul. I've looked for Paul in every government agency and he's not there. I'll keep looking, though. Just because my parents died doesn't mean Paul is dead."

Zach nodded. "That probably wasn't his real name."

"I thought of that, too."

"Want to talk about yesterday?"

She turned and put her cup on the table, then sat, and Zach joined her. "Sometimes keeping their secrets gets to me." She waved her hands as if erasing what she'd just said. "I hate keeping their secrets. They didn't give me that same courtesy to have someone to talk to and share their lives with. All that I know is by digging into files that are just now becoming open. Through those, I'm able to piece together their movements based upon what was happening then in the world.

"I ask Flora, but she's no help. Kay didn't say much,

but each of those gold cups represents a place they've been."

"I'd never get rid of a cup or that room."

"I'm tired of living here in a home with no love, Zach. I loved Rob and LaKota's house. There were toys everywhere. The babies were talking to each other in their baby language. I felt like I could fall asleep over there. Your brothers were on the grill, you were constantly getting into things and your sisters were talking to each other. That's a family."

"Baby, it has nothing to do with the house and everything to do with the people in the house. I have a house and I never go there."

"Why?"

He shrugged. "Nobody's home."

They both laughed. "I feel the same way. Where's your house?"

"Around the corner from my brother's house. I don't have the same quality of furniture or anything like in their houses. I've been there twice in the past month, just to make sure the landscaper cuts the grass. I love being around the family. And when I'm on a case, I'm one hundred percent on it."

She put her hand on his knee. "I know exactly how you feel. I loved having them here. So you're a dressed-up homeless fella, huh?"

"You got jokes, is that it?"

Her gaze became distant. Without trying, she began to look more like her mom, Kay, than Kim.

"I used to wish my father had cheated on my mother. I used to pray someone would come to me and say they were my sister or brother. But he was so loyal to her. When that car crash took them, I hated their guts. I hated them for not loving me enough to take me with them. I kept that room closed up for years. Not even Flora was allowed in there."

"What changed that?"

"Kay. Mum. I said aloud, I need to call Mum, and I realized she wasn't alive. I flew into a rage and unlocked the door. I raged at that painting. I told her how selfish she was, how angry she'd made me for never celebrating my birthdays. My first period. My first boyfriend, my first heartbreak. She was never there for me. So often, my calls to her went unanswered. She loved this damn government more than she loved me. And I told all that I knew about her. Herbert's telling took some time, but he didn't escape."

"What are you going to do now?"

"It's time to tear down those walls. I'm tired of walking past those rooms."

Zach caressed her hand. "Herbert's room doesn't show up on any blueprints of this house."

Kim nodded. "Honey, you've heard about the Underground Railroad. This house is a piece of history. Herbert's room housed slaves who were passing through. He converted it himself."

Zach's eyes widened. "No—what? You're for real?"

Kim nodded. "It's been unofficially confirmed. I'll never sell this house, but I want to tear down those walls. Eventually, when I die, I want to leave the house to a family member or the Historical Society. It's a living piece of history."

She glanced up at the clock and still hadn't removed her hand from his. "I know I was a hot mess last night, but I do remember everything I said. I do love you, Zach. You don't have to love me back."

She rose. Zach took her by the waist and brought her down onto his lap.

"Zach, you don't have to say it back to me."

"Hush, Kim." She didn't look at him, her fear so apparent. As if she didn't deserve love.

"Zach—" Slowly, he tipped her back in his arms and kissed her until she understood that she was the love of his life.

"Stop telling me what I have to do. I can love you if I want to, woman."

He let her sit up and held her close. She caressed the back of his head, her leg jumping. "You do?"

He nodded. "Love can be very calm one minute, and hot and passionate the next, baby."

"I like this," she said. She squeezed him and held him tightly. "I like this a lot. Let's go to the boat today."

He didn't say anything. That was so risky. He'd have to clear it with the team and he didn't want to make another mistake.

"We'll see."

She sat back and looked at him. "You serious?" Her legs jumped in excitement. "We can have a picnic. I do great baskets."

"You're also a great judge. You have court in ninety minutes."

"You've got me down here making out with you and being neglectful of my job."

"We aren't in a short supply of criminals. They're going to be there. But you'd better run."

She stopped moving and cupped his face. Zach laced his fingers around her waist. "I've never been happier and more scared in my whole life."

"I understand." Making her happy scared the words out of him. "It scares me, too."

Her eyes slid closed. "Yes, I know. We'll talk more later."

Tenderly, their lips met before she hurried up the stairs.

When she was out of hearing range, he called Rob. "We've got a situation."

Chapter 15

Kim was glad to be out of court and she wondered why the feeling was becoming more prevalent. She was beginning to hate her job. Going to the boat had been on her mind all day. She put her arms over her stomach and bent over, her eyes closed. "My stomach hurts."

Helplessness consumed Zach. "Baby, you're stressed out. Stop thinking. I'm not going anywhere. We're going to catch this lady. Clark is back."

"I know. I'm thrilled about that. But something's going to happen. I feel it." She exhaled and sat up, looking out the window. The traffic lights were all green against the cloudy night sky.

They pulled up to the gate and Kim showed her ID and admittance pass. Driving to the parking lot closest to her dock, she felt calmer the closer they drew to her yacht. This may be what the doctor ordered to shake her mellow mood. She'd lost her passion for law today. She'd come upon people who'd blamed her before, but never those who wanted her dead and were so close to killing her. What did her life mean?

"We can park on the right. My baby, *Pride and Joy,* is down there."

Kim grabbed the groceries while Zach got their overnight bags and provisions. One of the local guys had already gassed up the boat for her, so all they had to do was cast off.

"Do you know how to sail?" she asked, keeping her voice down out of respect for the boats that were already docked for the night.

"I'm pretty sure I'm a better sailor than you," he bragged.

Kim swung a bag of groceries and hit him in the butt. "I don't think so. I got the best grade in sailing camp last year."

Zach laughed and boarded the yacht, turning to help her down. "You didn't say sailing camp, did you? I've owned six boats since I was twenty, and I still own two."

Kim stuck her tongue out at him. "You owned six because you let four sink." He took the bags and set them on the floor, then pulled her to him and kissed her tart tongue.

"There's only one way to cure a bad mood," he said, kissing her face and ears. He nuzzled her neck and cheeks.

"What is it?" she asked, not ready to shake her evening blues.

"Making love," he said, "under the clouds. That always makes me feel better."

"I've never done that."

"Well, that's going to change tonight. Let's cast off and get bare-assed naked under the sky."

"Okay."

Zach shook his head, laughing at Kim. "I've got a hundred dollars that says you're not going to do it."

"Get ready to lose a hundred bucks."

Kim took the food to the full-size kitchen, then helped Zach loosen the boat from its moorings. He started the engine and drifted out of the slip and into open water. They sailed for about fifteen minutes, until the lights from the dock were speckles dappling on the horizon.

The tension eased from Kim's body with each breath. She walked up behind Zach and wrapped her arms around him. "Can we stay here forever?"

"Of course we can, but you'd get bored, baby. Looking at me all the time. I'm not that interesting."

"I have money. We could travel. We'd never have to do the same thing twice. We could go to Africa. We could live there part-time and live here part-time."

Zach gently pulled Kim around to face him. "What's the matter, baby? You're rattled and you're letting what's happened get to you."

"Of course I am. Hearing in no uncertain terms that no matter what I've done in my life, no matter how good I've been to people, the sacrifices I've made, how I've fought for victims' rights I would have been killed because the guilty hate me. That hurts me. It makes me question my values and all that I've thought important. Why do I do this if my life is so insignificant?"

"Your life has value, Kim."

"I know that, but to whom?"

"To me."

"That's sweet, but it has to mean more to me, I'm realizing. The Baxters, Franklin and this crazy woman would have killed me and my memory would have lasted as long as my eulogy."

"Baby, stop this sad talk. Come lie down with me." The lake water was a little choppy, but Zach wanted to keep her above deck because he'd heard there was going to be a fireworks show, despite the cloudy night.

He ran below deck and grabbed the blankets he'd brought, then carried everything, along with a bottle of champagne, up the stairs to find Kim looking into the distance, while rubbing her arms. He put the champagne down and wrapped her in the blanket. Kim turned to him and closed her eyes. "I just want to rest. I just want everything to be over."

"It is, baby. We're anchored in the middle of the lake. Nobody knows we're out here. Go to sleep. You're safe."

"If I don't take my clothes off, do I still owe you a hundred dollars?" she murmured.

Zach lightly squeezed her bottom. "You bet your sweet ass you do."

Kim giggled and fell asleep.

The sound of cracking glass awoke Zach, the odor of melting plexiglass making him cough. Kim was still sound asleep. Zach reached for his phone, but didn't get an answer. He jumped up and he heard a splash and watched a figure swim toward shore.

"Kim, wake up! Kim!" He shook her and she still didn't respond. He saw that the champagne had been opened but was still full, so the smoke must have gotten to her.

He carried Kim on his back, the phone in his hand, going to the yacht's radio.

"Mayday, Mayday, this is *Pride and Joy,* ablaze, uh—" He remembered their coordinates and gave their exact location. "I have aboard Superior Court judge Kimberly Thurman, who is not responding. Mayday!"

"Your Mayday has been received and the U.S. Coast Guard is responding. Can you get to safety?"

"Yes," he coughed, his time limited.

Zach fastened Kim's safety vest, then his own.

"Zaaach," she moaned, coughing.

"Thank you, Lord!"

He opened the hatch beneath the boat. It was risky, but he couldn't take her through a wall of fire. He was going beneath it. He heard Hugh on the phone and Zach said, "Come get us. We're going in." He gave their coordinates and dropped the radio.

He strapped the scuba mask on to her face, one on to his and he pulled her in.

The water was hot, and Kim nose-dived to escape the heat. The lake had been built on top of a town, so she didn't want to go too deep, but she wanted to escape the hot water. Zach had been smart, tethering them together. They swam in unison in the dark, their strokes even and quick. Neither looked back at the boat, but Kim was sure they had to get away quickly.

Faster was all her brain registered. Something ripped into her leg and pain seared up to her hip, but she didn't stop the even strokes that would take her to safety. She could see nothing. She just kept swimming. Years of swim training came back to her. While growing up in Switzerland, she'd swum nearly every day. She was good at this. She would not die. She would not let Zachary die.

She'd been about to give up earlier, but now whoever had done this had made her angry. She was going to get them. She was going to get this person and end their path of destruction in her life.

Her hand touched sand first and she tugged the rope, signaling Zach to swim her way. He came toward her and they crawled ashore. His finger touched her lips and he signaled her to be quiet. She couldn't talk anyway. Her breathing was ragged, her chest heaving. They didn't know where the perpetrator was. Zach helped her pull off her mask. His lips touched her ear. "You okay? Burned?"

Kim felt his mouth, his chest heaving against hers. "Nothing too bad," she wheezed. "You?" she asked, helping him remove his mask from around his neck where he'd pushed it.

"Nothing I can't handle."

The boat blazed in the center of the lake and Zach watched it with his fist to his mouth as if he wanted to yell. "I'm going to kill whoever is trying to kill you. I'm going to kill them."

Red lights appeared at the top of the hill and the Hood insignia beamed into the sky. The Crawford crest was also beamed into the sky on the other side of the lake. Chills ran all over Zach's body. The cavalry was there.

"How did they know?" she asked quietly, wiping her scraped hands.

"They somehow must have heard the Mayday. Can you walk? They're going to turn this lake upside down if we don't get to them in ten minutes."

"I can walk. Zach, I just had the boat serviced. There was nothing wrong with it. The security cameras will tell us something."

On their feet, they started walking, arms supporting one another.

"I'm sure they're already on it. Let's get to the rest of the family. Come on."

They began to walk up the hill toward the crest.

Ben saw Zach first and ran toward him, catching his brother, whose leg had been badly gashed. "Nothing is simple with you, is it?"

"I guess not, bro. I'm killing that mother—"

"Whoa," Rob said, lifting Kim off her feet. "Her leg, Zachary. Let's get her downtown to Grady. Hugh, get on the horn to Dr. Shayla Crawford. We may need a burn unit."

Hugh called the Crawfords, who were on the other side of the lake with the coast guard. The ambulance sirens were heard within seconds. "I'm good," Kim said. "What's wrong with Zach?"

"Nothing. His leg is a little messed up. Nothing to worry about," Ben said, not wanting to tell the truth. The gash was significant.

"I'm good, Kim," Zach said. "She's going to worry," he signed to Ben, who was blocking him from seeing Kim. "Let's roll. What's the coast guard saying? Did they catch anyone?"

"No, but the Crawfords were up here celebrating Nick and Jade's anniversary and they saw a woman coming up with scuba diving equipment. Then your boat went up in flames. They put the numbers together, and now they've galvanized a manhunt that's out of control," Rob told them.

"I always liked them," Zach said, taking the bandages from the ambulance attendant and wrapping his own leg. "They were always my type of people." He compressed the gash and wrapped the wound. "Enough of this namby-pamby nonsense. Time to go hunt some coward ass! Who's with me?"

"Zach, our agents, Crawford team, the GBI and the marshals are looking for this person. We're taking you to the hospital and then back to the house."

"What about me?" Kim asked.

"You're going with us, Judge. You're not safe alone." Rob watched the paramedic work on her leg and hands.

"Ma'am, your blood pressure is elevated. We're taking you to Grady because of the burns. A helivac is standing by now."

"I don't need one."

"Ma'am, I'm following orders. Obviously someone

said you do, so please lie down and enjoy the ride to the helivac."

"Rob," she said, reaching out her hand as he climbed into the ambulance with her.

"Don't worry, sugarplum. I'm with you all the way."

"Where's Zach?" Rob smiled at her as the ambulance pulled away.

"He's on his way to Grady, too. He's going the long way, though."

"What's that mean?" she asked, trying to see but unable to.

"Ben is chasing him, because he doesn't like hospitals and he doesn't want to go. Then Hugh will trip him. Yep. Just happened. He'll be sedated, and then he'll be good to go." Rob chuckled. "He's a crazy kid."

"It's all my fault that he's hurt. I asked to come here and he was trying to make me happy."

"So it's my fault," Rob told her. "I approved this little trip to the lake. He called me this morning when you went up to get dressed for work. So if someone has to take responsibility, it will be me. Everyone is going to the hospital and everyone is going to be fine."

At the hospital, they were treated by the Crawfords and a team of doctors who were highly trained in the burn unit. Kim's were the most severe, and she stayed there overnight.

When she awoke the next morning, she was visited by every Hood in the family and then every Crawford who'd been at the lake. They praised her ability to withstand the heat of the water and swim the three quarters of a mile to shore, and invited her back anytime to use their boat.

Kim was touched beyond belief. Where had these people been all her life?

For a few more days, Kim slept in Rob and LaKota's home, listening to the family noises they made. DaKota talked to her daddy and mom, and Zach when he rode her around on his back like a horse.

He said little to Kim, but at night he'd curl around her and sleep, nightmares plaguing him.

Kim tried to sleep, but she was so envious of the loving couple and their baby that she couldn't. In the sleepless hours, she'd strip and climb back into bed, and Zach would palm her breasts in his sleep and finally settle down.

On the fifth morning, she was finally feeling human and ready to go home. Kim staggered to the kitchen for coffee and turned on the news. The yacht fire was still the top news story, and Kim's name was still plastered on every channel. Her most recent case had garnered lots of attention, but tied together, she'd made the national news.

Kim kept calling her office to empty her cellular voice mail because her phone had been destroyed in the fire, when she got a call from her phone company. They offered to have two phones delivered to her.

Kim accepted and set off a firestorm when she gave them the address to her office.

Zach was surly.

She couldn't conduct business without those phones,

but explaining to an angry man didn't matter when he was ready to fight over anything.

"Kim, you put us all in jeopardy—"

"By telling the man how to get to my job to drop off the phones?"

"Clark will handle that. You could have waited."

Kim came into the bedroom dressed in her hospital scrubs. "I couldn't. I needed my phones so I can stay in touch with the office. Something could go wrong."

"Just where do you think you're going?" he asked, as she put on her new eye shadow that made her look sexier than she should have in a nurse's uniform.

"I want to climb into bed with you," she said, "but I took another lady's shift at the hospital. I've been here for five days. I need to start getting back into society. I've imposed enough. I'm going home today."

"I don't want you to go."

"Sweetheart, is that why you stopped talking to me?"

"You should have seen how you looked when they put you under to scrape that skin off your legs."

Tears sprang to her eyes. "I know. Stop," she said, her voice cracking. "I've been here. I know what you're saying, but keeping me hidden won't save me. I have to be in the world to bring this person out. Please don't get so upset with yourself that you forget why you're here. Get her or him or whoever this is."

Kim wanted to climb into bed with Zach, who looked lost with that big bandage on his leg.

He was sitting on the side of the bed, with his socks in his hand.

"Hugh needs to see us. It's about the helicopter that's been over your house."

"Okay," she said. "Right now?"

"Yes. In the kitchen."

Kim walked into the kitchen with Zach at her side. She recognized the Hoods and two other faces. Nick Crawford and his wife, Jade Houston.

Jade crossed to her and hugged her. "How are you, Judge Thurman? You gave us quite a scare."

"I'm doing well and it's Kim, please. Commander," she said to Nick.

"Your Honor," he said, never breaking protocol, and she understood this about him.

Kim sat down and turned to Hugh. "We had the hardest time finding out information about the helicopter that was over your house. You indicated to us that you thought it might have been about an old boyfriend who was into reality TV."

"Yes. That isn't the case, I take it?"

"No," Hugh replied. "I've worked for the government in various capacities over the years, and there are things that I'm privy to that regular citizens aren't. This helicopter didn't have any markings, no known identifying numbers, which immediately said government to me. Only, I couldn't get any information on it from anyone."

Kim looked down. "I see. Well, I appreciate you trying."

"Your Honor," Nick spoke quietly, "Hood asked me to get involved because you were in danger. Without giving too much classified detail, the surveillance was done by CIA. And it wasn't to harm you, but to ward off harm. Your father was owed favors by several people, who promised to protect you. They were returning the favor and have been for the past several months, since you pulled a case that was just recently closed. Have you watched the news today?"

"No, Commander, I haven't."

"When you do, you will learn that last night while being moved to different prisons, Lieutenant Franklin was murdered, as was Mr. Bryson."

Kim's eyes squeezed shut as she digested the information. "Is there anything else?"

"The whereabouts of Attorney Phinney and his family is unknown."

"And the prosecutor?"

"Has been moved to a safe place."

"Anything else, sir?"

"Surveillance of your home has ended. They said that your father had a mean golf swing, as well."

Kim covered her mouth and bent over, swallowing her tears.

"My parents were spies for the U.S." She hiccuped back tears she couldn't shed. "I was educated in Switzerland. They died in a car crash when I was sixteen. I became a judge because I thought I could change the world, but I just don't have a passion for it anymore."

"Ma'am, you've done good work. It's time to think about yourself," Nick Crawford told her.

Kim stood taller. "Thank you all so much. Commander and Mrs. Crawford, thank you for these answers. I know now that they loved me. I always wondered."

Kim accepted a powerful embrace from Jade. "Don't ever wonder again. They did."

The commander embraced her, too. "Don't let doubt undo what's been done here. These people care about you. Don't walk away from this."

Kim nodded, but felt herself pulling away. "Thank you."

Zach had her coat and Hugh had the truck running. "We don't need all this. If you take me home, I can get my car."

"Get in, Kim," Zach said, looking weary. "I'm going with you."

Hugh was quiet the entire ride to the hospital. "You two go up and I'll park."

Kim wished she'd taken a pain pill before leaving home, but she had forgotten to with all that had happened. She and Zach didn't speak on the elevator ride up to the neonatal unit, and she wanted to reach for him but couldn't. She'd learned so much about her family and about herself. The Hoods and the Crawfords were the epitome of family and she wanted what they had. What she'd worked for meant nothing. How could she reinvent herself as just Raquel Wheeler or just Kim Thurman?

They stepped out on the fourth floor and the quietness felt uneasy. They walked down the hall to the unit and Kim hoped there were babies to rock. She needed the comfort.

"Where will you be?" she asked Zach.

"Right over here," he said, indicating the wall where he usually stood for the entire hour. He could watch the elevator, the stair exit and the neonatal entrance and exit.

"Would you like a chair?" she offered, knowing if she was in pain, so was he.

"No. Who is that?" he asked about the woman in the unit. Kim had seen her before, but not for several months.

"I've background checked everyone but her. Ask her to come out here."

Kim went inside the unit, while Zach called on his radio to Hugh.

He watched them for a minute, then turned away. Kim sighed and hung up her jacket. There was one baby, who was hollering her little head off. The other two volunteers said hi to Kim and she greeted them, but the lady she hadn't seen in a while kept her back turned.

Kim didn't care. She was tired of rude people.

They all ignored the precious little girl, so Kim walked over and read her card. She'd been abandoned five days ago, but Social Services hadn't come for her yet.

Kim picked her up and put her face close to the baby's. "Hello, precious one." The little girl's head snapped toward Kim's and she cried into Kim's ear. "I know," Kim said. "What happened?" The infant cried out her story of abandonment and sadness and fear. "Tell me more." She expressed her hopes for a good family, love and happiness. Her cries eased as Kim stroked her cheek and assured her of God's love.

"So we finally meet," the volunteer who hadn't spoken to her said. The floor nurse, Karen, walked in and the two volunteers who'd been there left to go home. Kim waved at them, but kept her attention on the baby.

Zach was back in position, but he walked away again.

"I'm Kim, and you are?"

"Just call me Shelby. So how do you feel when your life is changed forever, Kim?"

Alarm bells rang for Kim, but Shelby looked nothing like the woman from the ice cream store.

"Depends on if I like the surprise or not."

Shelby tapped her foot. "What if it's a bad surprise?" She squinted, then opened her eyes really wide. "You still don't recognize me?"

"No, Shelby. Should I?" Kim asked, trying to keep the baby out of harm's way. This lady emitted an aura of pure danger. Kim backed away from her and tried to put the rockers between them.

"Yes, you ruined my life. You should remember that." She laughed harshly. "My husband, Dewitt, was a nice man. He did a couple of bad things, but you locked him up and he was killed in jail. Murdered. I hate you. I left those notes on your gate to torture you. I tried to kill everyone in your life who you cared about, but you must have some lucky charm, lady. But your luck is running out."

"Get out of here right now. I've already called security."

"I don't care, Karen." Shelby sneered at her. "I don't

care about these babies or you. I care about revenge. And that's what I'm going to get right now."

Kim still had the baby in her arms and grabbed a bassinet and laid her in there as Shelby exited. Kim and Karen both tried to get Zach's attention, unsure what Shelby was going to do. She had her hand in her purse.

Kim had Hugh on the phone as Shelby engaged Zach in a conversation, then plunged a knife in his side. Kim screamed and dropped the phone.

Staggering a bit, he remained on his feet and punched her in the face, knocking her unconscious, as Kim hit the button to get out of the room.

Hugh rushed out of the elevator and took Shelby into custody as Kim and Karen gave aid to Zach.

Chapter 16

Xan and Rob were the only Hoods allowed to see Zach.

Kim sat in a private waiting room, her face on the conference table, crying her eyes out. She would accept no visitors until she could bring herself under control. So far it had been ninety minutes and she hadn't been in control at all.

Clark ran into the hospital, tanned and scared. His boss never cried and he was worried.

"Where is Judge Kimberly Thurman?"

He was shown the waiting room and slipped in quietly. She sat at the end of the table, her feet in UGG boots, leggings covering her legs, a long camisole and a wrap sweater. Her hair was all over her face. He ran to the bathroom and wet a towel, then guided her to the couch and made her lie down before applying the cloth to her face.

Gently he combed her hair. "Come on, love. Pull yourself together."

"If he dies, I'll never forgive myself."

"He's pulling through."

"He is?" she said, clinging to any thread of hope.

Clark swallowed his own tears. "Yes, darling. He is. Now, come on. It's time to change clothes and join the family."

The family embraced her as she barely contained her emotions. She held her stomach and prayed harder than she ever had in her life. When he was finally in recovery, she held back, not wanting to intrude. Zach demanded to see her.

When Zach saw Kim, she was a vision in creamy silk. There was stress in her eyes, but so much love, he couldn't do anything but try not to cry himself.

"They said I'm going to make it."

"I never doubted you would. I'm so proud of you. You were so brave." She wiped his eyes. "Don't cry, darling, or I'll start again, and Xan will make me leave. I can't stop her from doing one thing, Zach."

"I know," he managed, unable to take his eyes off Kim, the woman he loved. "Who was she?"

"A woman whose husband I convicted. He got killed in jail. She blamed me and she'd put tracking devices on everything I owned. Her husband was into surveillance stuff. Hugh would do sweeps, but never on my briefcase. She worked housekeeping in the building and had access."

"How'd she get us at the boat?"

"She just took her chance. We were supposed to drink the champagne, but didn't. I opened it, but it didn't smell right, so I let it breathe and fell back asleep. It would have killed us."

"Crazy lady," he said.

She ran her fingers down his arm to his hand. "I want you to come to my house and live with me. Make my home your home. Let me take care of you as you've taken care of me."

"Baby, you have a job."

She shook her head.

"What?" he said softly. "Why, Kim?"

"Because, my life has to have more meaning. I want to be loved and cherished and cared for, and care and cherish and love. Not the law, but someone."

"Me?"

She nodded.

"As my wife?" he asked. "Because I do things all the way. We can take our time because this is a whirlwind."

"Yes, we can," she said, smiling, kissing him softly. "Yes. I love you, Zach Hood."

"I love you, too, Kim Thurman Hood."

"Kim Hood is good enough for me."

Their lips met again in a kiss so sweet. "Then Kim Hood, it will be."

* * * * *

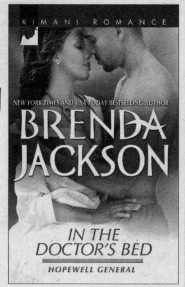

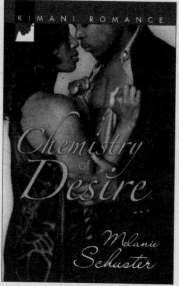

REQUEST YOUR FREE BOOKS!

2 FREE NOVELS
PLUS 2 FREE GIFTS!

KIMANI™
ROMANCE

Love's ultimate destination!

YES! Please send me 2 FREE Kimani™ Romance novels and my 2 FREE gifts (gifts are worth about $10). After receiving them, if I don't wish to receive any more books, I can return the shipping statement marked "cancel." If I don't cancel, I will receive 4 brand-new novels every month and be billed just $4.94 per book in the U.S. or $5.49 per book in Canada. That's a saving of at least 21% off the cover price. It's quite a bargain! Shipping and handling is just 50¢ per book in the U.S. and 75¢ per book in Canada.* I understand that accepting the 2 free books and gifts places me under no obligation to buy anything. I can always return a shipment and cancel at any time. Even if I never buy another book, the two free books and gifts are mine to keep forever.

168/368 XDN FEJR

Name _____
(PLEASE PRINT)

Address _____ Apt. #

City _____ State/Prov. _____ Zip/Postal Code

Signature (if under 18, a parent or guardian must sign) _____

Mail to the Reader Service:
IN U.S.A.: P.O. Box 1867, Buffalo, NY 14240-1867
IN CANADA: P.O. Box 609, Fort Erie, Ontario L2A 5X3

Not valid for current subscribers to Kimani Romance books.

Want to try two free books from another line?
Call 1-800-873-8635 or visit www.ReaderService.com.

* Terms and prices subject to change without notice. Prices do not include applicable taxes. Sales tax applicable in N.Y. Canadian residents will be charged applicable taxes. Offer not valid in Quebec. This offer is limited to one order per household. All orders subject to credit approval. Credit or debit balances in a customer's account(s) may be offset by any other outstanding balance owed by or to the customer. Please allow 4 to 6 weeks for delivery. Offer available while quantities last.

Your Privacy—The Reader Service is committed to protecting your privacy. Our Privacy Policy is available online at www.ReaderService.com or upon request from the Reader Service.

We make a portion of our mailing list available to reputable third parties that offer products we believe may interest you. If you prefer that we not exchange your name with third parties, or if you wish to clarify or modify your communication preferences, please visit us at www.ReaderService.com/consumerschoice or write to us at Reader Service Preference Service, P.O. Box 9062, Buffalo, NY 14269. Include your complete name and address.

KROM11B

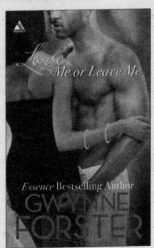

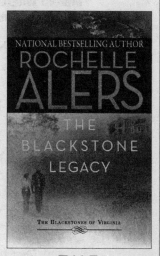

KPBJWR